Juggling Truths

Unity Dow

DOUBLE STOREY
BOOKS

This book is dedicated to my children Cheshe, Tumisang and Natasha to whom I have said before:

Trudge not through life, leaving ugly gashes,
Tiptoe not through life, leaving half-formed impressions,
Tread gently, lovingly; leave graceful heart prints,
Love the Earth, for she loves you so.

And to whom I say:

Leave a smell,
Leave a sound,
Leave a touch,
Leave a taste,
Leave a glimpse,
Leave an essence that is uniquely you,
Leave graceful heart prints.

Published 2004 in southern Africa by Double Storey Books,
a division of Juta & Co. Ltd, Mercury Crescent, Wetton,
Cape Town, South Africa

First published in Australia by Spinifex Press in 2003

ISBN 1-919930-41-8

Printed in South Africa by ABC Press, Epping, Cape Town

CHAPTER 1

My name is Monei Ntuka and this is the story of my childhood in the village of Mochudi, in the then British Bechuanaland Protectorate, in the mid to late sixties. It is, of course, not the whole story of my youth, for didn't my grandmother Mma-Tsietsi, mother of my father, tell me many times, 'A tongue can talk until numb with fatigue, but it can never tell the whole story'? And didn't she gently admonish me, when I would go on and on, saying, 'Child of my child, a good story teller knows when to stop, just as a dreamer knows when to wake up.' In any event, a look at self can never be a full stare; it has to be a series of glimpses.

Through the village a river flowed, bringing lots of life – fish in its waters and wild spinach along its banks – and around the village, hills stood, solid and reliable. The river also brought bilharzia and occasionally it claimed a young life, but one would not guess that from all the frolicking in the river that we did. On the Phuthadikobo Hill a one-eyed snake lived to protect the village and only the Chief could feed it. At night its eye could be seen shining down from the hill, which only a fool would climb at night. Beyond the hills were the lands, where we ploughed maize, millet, sorghum, watermelons, beans, sweet reed and many other foods. Beyond the lands were the cattle posts, the land of men and boys, where the cattle were kept and boys learnt to be men and men lived quietly missing their women and daughters. We lived a semi-nomadic life. From June to October we lived in the village proper, commemorating deaths and celebrating births and marriages and the women decorated *lapa* and house walls. Men would sit under trees in the mornings, enjoying their wives' brews eyeing

1

their toddlers and privately planning their next children. 'Your son is old enough to have a younger sibling; are you doing anything about it?' one would whisper to a brother, friend or cousin. 'This boy is too young to wean!' the mother might respond if she overheard the whisper. Or then she might agree that perhaps the boy should be weaned and that perhaps the next time they might be lucky and have a girl.

Occasionally men assembled at the village *Kgotla* to discuss weighty village matters, such as whether this or that cousin of the Chief should be given a ward to head. Or the District Commissioner (the Queen's representative, local magistrate and general main man for all things colonial) might address them about a visit of some anthropologist who would be coming to study their ways. Still, the Dutch Reformed Church missionaries might berate them for not encouraging their children to go to church. All these things they would tell to their wives around the evening fires as porridge bubbled and bean leaves boiled in front of everyone.

In October the Chief declared the ploughing season open and the whole village emptied out to the lands, scattered around the outskirts of the village and sometimes up to fifteen kilometres away. The move to the lands was an exciting exercise, involving a cacophony of banging pots, clucking chickens, children under foot and always resulted in disagreements between the husbands and wives. The women trying to load yet another extra pot on to the ox wagon and the men arguing that there was no more space and, 'Shouldn't you have packed all this yesterday? We will not get to the lands before sunset, at this rate!' The argument might also be about whether a son was old enough to make the journey by foot, driving the goats, with older boys. 'He is too small to walk with the older boys. Please let him ride in the wagon,' the mother would plead. 'You are turning him into a girl before my very eyes!' Amongst the confusion of shouts of goodbyes to neighbours, last minute items to load and the general excitement of the move, the boy might still slip into the wagon.

At the lands the men would harness the oxen and till the land, while women repaired hut roofs, *lapa* and hut walls and cooked large amounts of food for their men. It was important to keep the men fed and strong and perhaps the biggest error a woman could possibly commit around ploughing time would be not to have a meal ready on time for the men sweating in the October/November sun. Having ploughed the fields, the men would move on, taking the cattle with them, this time to the cattle post, at which they would stay and tend the cattle. Often they left the goats behind and a boy or two to help the women with them. With the rains, the livestock would start to have kids and calves and milk would start to flow and the children's behinds would fill out, to the joy of the mothers.

In December, just before Christmas, young men, donning the latest style hats and strutting like proud cockerels would arrive from the gold mines in South Africa. By then the fields would be green with promise and different types of wild spinach and berries would be flourishing everywhere. We, the children, would eat, run errands and play; eat, run errands and play. In the evenings, in spaces cleared for that purpose, there would be choir practices, this in preparation for the all-night competitions that took place from the afternoon of the eve of Christmas to the morning of Christmas.

'Don't believe a man shortly arrived from the mines, he is full of promises and longing. Wait until the crops are in and see if he still sings the same song,' my grandmother declared, one such night as we sat around the evening fire, while my sisters got ready for a choir practice. 'Don't believe a man who does not mention sending his uncle to your family,' my mother added.

'It's only a choir practice,' my sister Keneilwe said, sounding embarrassed.

'It's always something innocent to start with,' both women would chorus.

'What promises and longing?' I asked.

'Promises of marriage and longing for female company,' my grandmother explained.

'Go to bed, Miss Long-Ears, you are too young to still be up,' Keneilwe threatened.

'I don't want to know about men's promises and longings,' I responded hoping that, with the declaration of disinterest, I would be allowed to stay up longer.

'Good, now go to bed, Nei,' my mother said. I should have

stayed out of matters that did not concern me, but it was too late and my mother had spoken, so I went to bed.

With young men from the mines flush with money and longing for female company, marriage proposals were made along sandy lanes with the earth erupting with leaves, flowers and berries, and with yellow butterflies fluttering around. Some of the proposals would be repeated by uncles in earnest later in the village, when such matters could be seriously addressed, but many ended up merely stolen kisses and hands held in the bush.

In April, the husbands would come back to the lands, bringing a few of the cows and their calves, and dispatch the boys to the cattle post and move young kids out of the mother's hut to sleep with older siblings or with grandparents. There would be even more milk and sour milk would be made. The sweet reeds, watermelons, beans, and many other *letlhafula* foods would be ready and the days would be one long string of feasting. A goat might be killed if the rains were particularly good and the herd thriving. A goat would be killed anyway, if there were a new mother in the compound, good rains or not. Then there would first be fried liver and tripe, then fresh meat and then endless days of biltong. The goodness of the year was always gauged by the health of the children – visible rib cages would bring clucks of concern from the mothers and sad shakes of heads from the fathers. During the day, the men would repair the field bush fences, hut beams or the goat kraals. They might also use the days, as the women watched the field, chasing birds and hoeing out weeds, to tan leather and make harnessing ropes. If they were so skilled, they might carve extra bowls, pestles, mortars, spoons and yoking tools. When the rains were good, April became a month of much whistling by men and humming by women. We children played and helped and played and helped. At night we listened to stories by my mother and grandmother and then we collapsed with exhaustion, with sweat caked to our chests and foreheads and earth caked to our feet, for there was always something to do or a game to play. Once a week we got a scrubbing, which we hated if it was done at home but loved if it was done at the well. At the well, a wash ended up as a swim and a game, but at home, with water brought in one bucket at a time, the washing took on a rather business-like character.

Once I started school though, when I was about seven years old, this rhythm was interrupted for I had to stay in the village during school term and to walk to the lands during weekends and school holidays. My life then became split into two realities and it often seemed that they were not complementary. For example, at home, at the lands and at the cattle post, the river that flowed through our village was called Ngotwane but at school I learned that it was called Notwani. And while I was a Motswana at home, at the lands and at the cattle post, I was a Bechuana at school. These were just a few of the truths that I had to juggle during my seven years of primary school. Later, I started to make up my mind about things, but this is not the story of later.

My parents Tsietsi and Marato had six children who were named Leruo, Keneilwe, Mmadira, Noka, Monei and Keletso. Leruo, meaning livestock, was so named to signify hope of prosperity – a kraal full of cattle. Keneilwe, meaning 'I have been given', was a name signifying gratitude to God and the ancestors. Obviously, although many more children were hoped for, a boy followed by a girl meant having one of each and both had to be grateful. The third child, Mmadira, 'the mother of enemies' or 'the woman of enemies', was named after a great-grand-aunt. The great-grand-aunt had been born during some war with the Ndebele people. It is said that she was kidnapped, never to be heard of again, by an enemy regiment. Since then her name had been given to any descendant child who was born with a birthmark on her left thigh and Mmadira had such a mark. My brother Noka, which meant river, was so named because the Notwane River, which flows through our village, broke its banks the year he was born. When it receded, there was plenty of wild spinach, fish and birds nested in its huge *medubu* trees. This explained his *matlhaletso* or love or comfort names, Thepe and Ramedubu. I was named Monei, 'the one who gives'. Like Keneilwe, it is a name that signifies gratitude for the birth of a child. It was also decided, on the basis of the shape of my eyes and my dimpled cheeks, that I was destined to be generous and good-natured. Everybody called me Nei, except, of course, when they were angry with me. Then, when I was twelve years old and had been settled into life as the last born, Keletso was born and I would have happily strangled that child. Even her name, Keletso – 'she who has been wished for', was enough to throw any sibling into a jealous rage.

Of course, we all had plenty of other names, but these were the names that got used most times. For example, I had at least three other names – my father had named me Lelegaisang, after his own mother, the same grandmother had named me Naniso after my grandaunt, and an uncle had named me Ngwedi for having been born a full-moon night. The three would occasionally call me by the name they had chosen for me or by nicknames generated from those names, but generally, they too called me Monei or Nei.

I remember one Saturday morning in September towards the end of my first year in school, when I would have been about seven or eight years old, my friend Kabo and I watched forlornly through the only window from inside a rondavel at Kabo's compound. The rain was coming down in solid sheets, pounding the earth and I could see my mother hurrying into our yard next door, dripping wet. She had a bundle of firewood on her head and she had been caught in the rain. I shouted to her that I was at Kabo's, so she would not worry about me and she waved back to acknowledge that she had heard me. There were streaks of lightning and Kabo's mother had hidden the only mirror in the house under a pile of blankets. Lightning was attracted to mirrors and we could be struck and killed if such precautions were not taken.

The rain would not stop but we wanted to go out to play and our patience was running out. Being cooped up on a weekend day was not our idea of fun. We watched hopefully as the clouds pretended to disperse only to thicken and darken again.

'Let's chase the rain away,' I finally suggested.

'Should we?' Kabo asked looking around to see if anyone had heard my suggestion. We both knew that rain was precious but it seemed that we were getting too much of it.

'I'm sure we have had enough. Look, there are puddles every-where. It's been raining for two days! I heard my mother saying that the rain must stop or it will rot the seeds planted yesterday. I say we chase the rain away.' We had been watching the steady rain through the window, hoping that it would stop so we could get out of the smoky rondavel where Kabo's sister Norah was cooking the midday meal. The wet wood was not burning well and she had an

6

annoyed look on her face. The other children were playing a game involving a series of questions, and merciless tickling of whomever could not answer the question, and they seemed content to wait out the rain. The rondavel was smoky though, from damp wood and the confined space. Kabo and I had had enough. In any case, we were both angry with Norah for ordering us to stop singing in the house. Norah was always issuing orders and generally bossing us children around whenever we were alone with her.

Kabo looked around before answering, 'Okay. But we have to go outside to do it. Let's go behind the house.' As we tried to slip out, hoping that none of Kabo's siblings would want to know why we were going out in the rain, Selinah looked up and opened her mouth. Selinah was Kabo's four-year-old sister, and we were convinced that she had been born for the specific purpose of tormenting us with her demands for attention. She wailed when we did not include her in our play, she told on us if we went swimming in the river and she demanded our protection whenever she was under attack by her own playmates. So when her mouth opened I knew immediately that one of us had to act. I surreptitiously spat out the two-day gum I had been chewing and slipped it into Selinah's mouth and her eyes glinted gratefully. As she started chewing I smiled at her and patted her head, winked at Kabo and we went outside. She might have been four but she could be trusted not to swallow a piece of gum. She was not at all like Mmandisa, my cousin who had swallowed her sister's five cents, with the annoying and unpleasant result that the poor sister had had to follow her around until the coin made its appearance in the little girl's faeces. Her sister had been a day late in paying for her Girl Guide badge and had been caned for that. No, Selinah knew better than to swallow my gum. We had been told repeatedly that, if a child swallowed a piece of gum, the gum would blow up inside the child's stomach, killing the child. Kabo and I had discussed this piece of adult wisdom and we had agreed that it was nonsense but, still, we didn't want to find out. I planned to retrieve my gum later and I figured it was good for another day or so. I would have to think of something to give to Selinah or we could have a howling drama to deal with. Perhaps she would be happy if I painted her fingernails with my indelible pencil. Or perhaps I could promise her half my orange. Once a month we were given an orange at school. The next orange day would be the coming Wednesday so I very much doubted that Selinah would want to wait that long. I would have to go the nail-painting route, even though her mother would be very angry at that. I could always say Selinah cried for me to do it and that I painted her fingernails to stop her from crying. Selinah's tantrums were legendary, so I just might be believed. It would be the truth too.

Once outside, our brown bodies glistened as the rain rolled down our bare skin, for we were clad in *makgabe* and *tshega* respectively. My *makgabe,* a short string skirt, was new and had been presented to me by my grandmother, Lelegaisang or Mma-Tsietsi, as a present for staying in school. I had hoped to visit friends in the neighbourhood to show it off this weekend but the rain was spoiling my plans. Kabo's *tshega* was old and stiff. At the very least, it needed washing. He was not concerned about its state though.

We decided to make a wish to the rain before chasing it away. 'Rain, rain, make me grow, rain, rain make me grow,' we sang and skipped in the middle of the compound. Then we went to the back, took furtive looks around and, having assured ourselves that no one was watching, bent over, exposing our butts to the skies.

Having embarrassed the clouds, we ran back into the rondavel to watch them disperse. Within half an hour, the sun was re-asserting itself and the clouds were retreating. Two large rainbows appeared in the northern sky and we skipped out into the cool moist air and went to make rivers and huts with water and wet sand and to chase butterflies and make houses of sand. We had to make sure not to step onto and kill *Bana Ba Modimo,* Children of God. These bright red little mites that came out after the rains were a source of wonder to us. Their velvety look made them seem not only beautiful but also delicate. We knew that killing them deliberately was not permitted and stepping on one inadvertently called for making a circle around the dead insect and saying an apology to the ancestors. They came with the rains and that was evidence enough that they were sacred. We teased baby millipedes, making them roll onto their back and wriggle around in annoy-ance, until finally they would curl up. We chased butterflies and

8

tried to catch grasshoppers. We briefly discussed marriage to each other but just as quickly decided against it. We decided we could not survive the months of living apart when he would have to go to the cattle post while I was at the lands. We decided we would be friends forever and we would not marry anyone else.

No more than thirty minutes into our play, a shrill voice pierced the air, 'Snake! Snake! Snake!' Within seconds the neighbours were at the scene hurling stones and wielding sticks. Snakes were killed on sight and it was only much later before I learned that there are actually many harmless ones. When they were done stoning and beating the snake, a huge cobra lay writhing pathetically, its head smashed and its body punctured in many places. A man turned it over, exposing the underbelly and frightened gasps could be heard from the assembled children and some women. I backed away as I felt salty saliva filling in my mouth. I knew I would throw up if I stuck around to watch the writhing snake. I feared snakes, I still do, but I was appalled by the way they were killed. And I definitely did not want to see the underbelly of a snake. There was something frightening about that smooth, whitish long skin. I wished we had not chased the rain, then perhaps the snake would have stayed where it had been to start with. I felt partly responsible for the snake's brutal death. Still, I was relieved that it had been spotted and killed before it had bitten and harmed someone.

As I walked away Rra-Bina called after me, 'Nei, my wife, come here. Don't be afraid of the snake. It's dead, Nei.' I didn't know what to do. Rra-Bina, a man from a compound in the neighbourhood was an adult and therefore could not be disobeyed. But he was being playful, calling me 'my wife' as he always did. I was always embarrassed by this, but felt there was nothing I could do about it. Other girls seemed to enjoy such teasing but I did not. In fact, I hated his teasing intensely. Going back to Rra-Bina might be interpreted as accepting that I was his wife but ignoring an adult might be seen as rude. I decided to go with rudeness. I straightened my back defiantly, set my mouth in a pout and walked on, ignoring the calls and laughter from behind me.

'That wife of yours is stubborn,' someone joked and then laughed at his own observation. 'You must keep her in line.'

'No, she is just shy. Aren't you little Nei, my wife?' Rra-Bina called after me.

'Give her time, soon she will be running towards you not away from you,' someone added. I heard Kabo calling me back, inviting me back to our interrupted play but I ignored him.

Although I knew that the wife-calling was just jest, there were times when I was filled with some panic. Granted Rra-Bina was married and Bina, the son he was called after, was years older than I was. In addition, I was aware of only three men in the village who had more than one wife. But still the second wives were much younger than the men and the first wives. I was also very vaguely aware of a practice called '*go baa letlhokwa*' whereby an older man, even a married man, would select a girl child as his wife to be. Then, over the years, he would offer the child's family gifts of food, clothing for the child, firewood. When the child was ready for marriage, say at eighteen or so, he would then take her as his wife. I had attended only one marriage ceremony like that and the young bride had not seemed particularly happy. But then no bride I had ever seen had seemed happy; in fact, most looked down and cried. I had not heard any mention of any such arrangement between my parents and Rra-Bina, but still I wished he would not go around referring to me as his wife. And I wished my mother would not laugh it off the way she did. Even my brother Noka had started teasing me about it.

'Rra-Bina's wife! Rra-bina's wife!' Noka chanted as I re-entered the yard. There was nothing in my manner that suggested that I was paying Noka any attention at all. I walked on but Noka knew to get off my path. We had fought often enough for him to tell from the narrowing of my eyes and the creasing of my forehead that an attack was imminent. In fact, Noka called my pre-attack face 'puppy face' and when we were not fighting he would ask me to set my face in 'puppy face' mode, and I would oblige. And we had raced each other often enough to know that we were evenly matched, so he took a few steps back before continuing his chanting.

'I see Rra-Bina's wife! Rra-Bina's wife! I see Rra-bina's wife! Rra-Bina's wife is afraid of dead snakes! Rra-Bina's wife is a coward! What will Rra-Bina do with a coward?' Noka continued to chant from what he thought was a safe distance. Without breaking my stride, I bent over and picked up a hard clod of earth. I threw the clod at my brother and when it landed on his forehead it broke into a sandy cloud. Noka howled in response, announcing for all to hear that I had blinded him for life. He would never see again, he declared, thanks to his brutish sister.

'What's going on with you two?' my mother called from behind one of the houses.

'She has blinded me!' 'He is teasing me!' we chorused, each hoping to be heard above the other.

'Come here, both of you. And you! Stop howling like a little girl! Your friends can hear you and you will be the laughing stock of the whole neighbourhood! What boy howls like that?'

'But she has thrown sand into my eyes. I may never see again,' Noka's whining was winding down to quiet sniffles.

'Monei, how many times have I told you not to throw objects at other people? How many times? What are you? Some wild boy? Is that what you are? Do you want me send you off to the cattle post? Is that what you want? What girl goes around fighting boys?' Seeing that things were developing in his favour, Noka made the mistake of smiling and winking teasingly at me.

'Noka, since you don't know what to do with your time, go and get the goats. And when you bring them back, you will milk them without assistance! And if you milk Mmakotswana too much, starving that poor kid to death, I will kill you myself! And now go! And stop rubbing your eyes or you will indeed end up blind! And off you go! Now!'

'But *mma*, it's Rapula's turn to bring in the goats.' Rapula was a cousin who had been living with us since his parents had died in a lightning strike which it was generally agreed had been sent by Mmankwe, Rapula's father's lover. He was due to leave for Shoshong to go and live with a childless distant uncle and his wife. Numerous meetings had been held on the issue and a final decision had just been made – he was due to leave at the end of the year but, in the meantime, he had to help Noka with the goats. I was happy that Rapula would be leaving. Just as I felt sorry for him to be an orphan, he complicated my relationship with Noka, interfering in our quarrels and offering unsolicited sympathy to me whenever

Noka beat me. He was my age but, because he lived with us, I called him brother. When people asked who was older we both kept quiet. We would have to explain that we were siblings by blood but not by one woman and that his parents were dead. The explanation always brought tears to his eyes. I wanted Rapula to go to Shoshong to live with his new parents so he could take his sadness with him. I had even convinced Kabo to join me in a special secret prayer on the matter. Kabo didn't like praying, believing, as his grandfather did, that it was enough to wish something with your whole heart, and that praying out aloud was silly.

My mother regarded my brother and shouted at him, 'Are you challenging me? Don't answer back when I talk to you! Go! I am going to spit on the ground, and before the spittle dries, you better be back with all the goats, if you know what's good for you. If you come back with even one goat missing, you will spend the night in the kraal so you know how the missing goat feels! And as for you Monei, take a broom. I am looking away and when I look back, I want this whole yard swept clean! I don't want to hear or see any more fights between the two of you. What am I raising? A pair of bullocks? You make more noise than a pack of jackals, I declare!' Our mother went back to her grinding malt for the beer she would be brewing for her husband, relatives and friends in celebration of the new rainy season.

I was in the middle of my chore when who should come in but Rra-Bina and he immediately teased me, 'Oh my wife. You can sweep a whole yard! You are a proper little woman. I may have to marry you sooner than I thought!' For a split second I considered throwing the broom at Rra-Bina's smiling face. Instead I dissolved into tears throwing the broom away. I ran to my mother who looked up exasperated, 'Now what's the matter? Will you ever give me peace to finish one little task?'

I stomped my foot for emphasis and declared, still crying, 'I am not Rra-Bina's wife!'

My mother shook her head, threw her hands in the air and gave me an annoyed smile, 'Of course you are not. Are you still crying over what Noka said? Come on, Nei. It is just a harmless joke!'

'What's wrong with little Nei?' Rra-Bina asked pretending

innocence and fondling my head. I shrugged him off to avoid any further contact. 'Is she still upset by the killing of the snake?'

'No, she is crying because she does not want you to call her your wife! God knows every woman wants to be somebody's wife! And God help the man who marries this one, for he will have a leopard for a wife!'

'I am not a woman! And I am not a leopard!' I answered belligerently, but with eyes still brimming with tears. 'And I am not going to sweep the yard any more!' I sat down defiantly folding my arms for emphasis.

'Oh, little Nei, I was just playing with you. Don't be so upset. Will you make me some tea if I promise not to call you my wife any more?'

I looked at Rra-Bina and, noting the smile on his lips, I was not sure that I could trust his promise.

I stood up and faced Rra-Bina. Creasing my forehead to demonstrate the seriousness of the moment, I demanded, 'Swear by the red book at the Dutch Reformed Church that you will not call me your wife, ever!'

'Nei, you can't talk to Rra-Bina like that,' my mother remonstrated.

'I swear by the red book at the Dutch Reformed Church that I will never again call you my wife,' Rra-Bina answered, amused, although I was trying to put as much fierceness in my face as I could muster. He extended his pinky to seal the promise and I approached and hooked my own pinky around the extended finger. Rra-Bina sliced the fingers apart with his left hand with what I thought was mock seriousness. I had to make sure that he kept his promise so I added, 'Now if you break the promise you will be struck by lightning from a cloudless sky. Say you believe that!'

'Believe me, I will never risk *tladimothwana,* for lightning that strikes on a cloudless day is the most deadly. Now where is my tea?' I knew then that he was serious, so I skipped off, happy that I would never be Rra-Bina's wife, either in jest or in reality.

Once I was on the other side of the *lapa* wall, I crawled back to listen to the two grown-ups. I was certain they would make some comment on the matter when they thought I was out of earshot. I heard my mother half-seriously rebuking her neighbour for letting me talk to him like an equal. 'You can't let her talk to you like that. She will never know right from wrong. You must be firm with children if you want them to learn respect.'

Rra-Bina looked at my mother and answered with a smile, 'What about you? She has just told you she is not going to finish sweeping the yard and what did you do? Monei is a little leopard. You stroke her, she purrs. You tease her, she scratches. Yes, you have a leopard in that girl, Mma-Monei! The man who marries her will spend a lifetime trying to trim those claws! Good luck to him!' Rra-Bina stifled a laugh.

Later, when Noka brought the goats only to find the yard half-swept he was ready for another fight with me. 'Wife of Rra-Bina, why have you not done your chore?' He whispered to avoid getting into trouble with our mother.

'Wife of Rra-Bina is anyone stupid enough to ask irrelevant questions. In fact, I see a girl masquerading as a boy, right in front of me. All boys I know have shot at least one bird with their slingshots, but there is someone I know who has not. Perhaps Rra-Bina can take him as his wife!' I retorted. Noka shut up. He did not want further discussions about his shortcomings as a bird hunter. He had already had to fight a friend about that same topic only two days previously. And he had lost the fight, the evidence being a still-swollen knee, which he was hiding from our mother.

Within an hour, we had forgotten the earlier fights and we were taking turns to tell stories by the fire. When it was our grand-mother's time to tell a story, she told the story of Dimo, the great giant who was found in many Setswana stories. In all the stories, he stole children and, although in most stories he was chased away by some quick thinking man in the village, we all preferred the one story in which he actually died. Noka and I, like all the other children, feared Dimo and half-expected him to appear in reality one day to steal one of us. From the time we were around six years old, we had known that Dimo was a fictitious creation of the parents, used to silence children into obedience. But still, a story in which Dimo died ensured a night of sound sleep.

'It is said that a long, long time ago,' my grandmother started. 'All the village children met at the village well and they

14

encountered Dimo, head in the mud, buttocks in the air. The children had a brilliant idea, to play inside Dimo's buttocks.

"'Dimo's buttocks, open up!" they called out and indeed Dimo's buttocks opened. The children climbed in and played and played and played. "Dimo's buttocks, open up!" and the buttocks opened up again and the children climbed out into the sunshine. After a while, the children wanted to go back in to play, so once again they shouted, "Dimo's buttocks, open up!" In they went, to play in the dark recesses of Dimo's bottom. When they were tired of playing in the dark, they shouted, "Dimo's buttocks open up." But this time Dimo's anus would not open up. It remained shut and his tummy started to rumble. His heart beat thunderously and his breathing sounded like the August wind. The children were scared. They huddled in the dark, entreating Dimo's buttocks to open up. They cried and begged but Dimo's buttocks refused to listen. They promised never to engage in dangerous play again. They had no way of knowing if it was night or day outside.

'Then the father of one of the children, a man of great courage who had led men into war and had killed a lion, a leopard and a buffalo, using only an axe, was passing by when he saw huge buttocks pointing to the sky.

"'What monster is this that will chase the rains forever by exposing himself to the skies?" But on a closer look, the man saw that it was Dimo, head stuck in the earth and buttocks grotesquely exposed. As the man watched, he heard faint cries from inside Dimo's buttocks.

"'The children! The children!" he shouted. He ran into the village and called upon all able-bodied men to bring their axes. He himself brought the very axe he had used to slay a lion, a leopard and a buffalo and within hours the men had chopped Dimo's buttocks open and the children spilled out into the night, for the sun had long set. Mothers came to claim their children who all promised never ever to disobey their parents and happiness came to that village for many years. For Dimo had been killed.'

I loved these stories, but I loved even more, the private stories my grandmother told me.

CHAPTER 2

I was nine years old and in Standard One, my third year of primary school when I had Mrs Monyatsi as my teacher. There was general agreement, within the school and even beyond, that Mrs Monyatsi was the most vicious of all the teachers. Stories about her were told in whispers. She could use both hands to slap a face, so ducking was not just futile, it was not recommended as it would most definitely drive her insane. She pinched the armpits. She pinched the soft inner thighs. She pinched behind the ears. She pinched and pulled noses and ears. She struck the tips of fingers with the edge of a ruler. Sometimes she even spat. And she had been known to kick.

Mrs Monyatsi not only hurt her charges physically, but she humiliated them as well. Every year, she memorised not just the names of her pupils, but the names of each pupil's mother, as well as the names of the mother's mother. She had little interest in the paternal sides of her pupils' families. She had grown up in Mochudi and therefore she was privy to scandals and rumours not known to teachers who had come from other villages. She used this information, adding her own angles to it, in order to torment and embarrass her charges. Her tongue was deadlier than a black mamba's fangs, was the general consensus.

I had spent the December holidays worried that I would get Mrs Monyatsi as my class teacher. There were three Standard One teachers and I had hoped for Miss Lebekwa, a gentle, funny teacher, who used her cane reasonably. Or even Mr Dlodlo, a teacher who spoke Sesotho, which to us sounded like a very peculiar, as well as funny, version of Setswana. He called buttocks anuses, and when he was hungry, he said he was sleepy. Sesotho was clearly a reverse version of Setswana. All this we found amusing and he laughed good-naturedly along with his students. His preferred mode of punishment was inner-thigh pinching for girls and ear pulling for boys, which though painful, was nothing compared to what Mrs Monyatsi could think up and execute. He smoked in class and sipped a liquid he claimed was tea, but which was rumoured to be something else, from a flask he kept with him at all times. Mr Dlodlo was reputed to be lazy though, and his students did not do well in their end of year exams. Failing a standard could lead to repeating that standard, a thing that was not only embarrassing, but could earn one a series of thrashings. That is, a home thrashing, a thrashing by the Principal and a thrashing by the class teacher who had to suffer the pupil for another year. So Miss Lebekwa was my first choice, but I would take Mr Dlodlo if the toss were between him and Mrs Monyatsi.

When the sun came up on Christmas day, dancing and floating to celebrate the birth of Jesus Christ, I had made a silent prayer that I not get Mrs Monyatsi. Then just in case my first prayer was not answered, I said a quick second one, before the sun stopped spinning, that if I did get Mrs Monyatsi, that she did not find out about my great-great-grandmother. I had even seriously considered dropping out of school if I did get Mrs Monyatsi. My brother Noka had been taken out of school, after two years of primary school, to look after the family goats. The goats moved between the village, the lands and the cattle post, depending on the time of the year. Caring for goats was not generally compatible with going to school so he had had to leave school. He had therefore never had to face Mrs Monyatsi but he had promised to say a special prayer for me, to help me avoid Mrs Monyatsi's class. Either Jesus Christ did not hear my main prayer, what with all the wishes from so many people about so many things, or he could not help. There had to be at least forty unfortunate children destined for Mrs Moyatsi's class, no matter how Jesus Christ managed things. If Jesus failed to save me from Mrs Monyatsi, I just hoped that he could at least grant me my other prayer. It occurred to me though, that the doubts I had about Jesus, and what he could or could not do, may have had something to do with his not granting my prayer. My grandmother was very wise; the evidence was her advanced age, her impressively wrinkled face, her two petticoats, and hair that was always covered with a head scarf. She had once whispered to me that if Mary had been pressed, she would have told a better story about Jesus' totem. She hadn't elaborated and at that time I had not been too clear about where babies came from, but it raised, in my mind, questions about Jesus' identity. Clearly, it seemed, if Mary had lied about Jesus' totem, no one knew who he really was and that could mean that he was not the Son of God. I had tried to push this doubt from my mind as I prayed that Christmas morning, but the problem is that you can't hide your thoughts from God and if it is His Son's identity you are questioning, your prayers are doomed from the start.

When my first prayer was not answered, I decided to call on my ancestors to help as well. I knew that Father James did not approve of this practice, calling this 'ancestors and spirits worship'. Which seemed strange because he prayed to Jesus, who was long dead, and the Holy Spirit. Jesus was not even his ancestor, from all accounts. It was with this same half-belief and half-hope that I was to approach horoscopes when I discovered them in high school. Without any proof, I was never really sure of my date of birth. I doubt that anyone in my class, except perhaps Maureen and Simon, who had been born at Deborah Retief Hospital, were certain about their dates of birth. And definitely Berka Solomon Moatshe, who was delivered by Mr Berka Solomon, in a white van after his mother died in childbirth in Johannesburg. Berka Solomon's mother had been a housemaid for the Solomons, and they were indeed very special people, to have taken the trouble to bring the baby across the border. There were papers on his birth, one titled Birth Certificate as well as a letter bearing the title 'Travel Document – Black Orphaned Infant – Male'. Berka Solomon was very proud of this documentation evidencing his origins. Rose must have had a birth certificate although she never said and we never asked. Otherwise almost everyone else was born at home to parents who could neither read nor write. Dates of birth had been pure estimations. Some were even the creations of the teachers, because the class register had a space for such details.

As it turned out, five pupils from our class did drop out of school and amongst the five was Lorraine, a beautiful, amazingly clean and tidy girl who said very little in or out of class and seemed to learn even less. Lorraine had joined our class the previous year, during the last term of Sub B, from South Africa. Lorraine had smooth golden skin, closely cropped hair, new shoes, new uniform and a neat nicely fitting cape and blue tights. The smoothness of her feet, exposed very seldom as she was not into bare-foot games like skipping and hide-and-seek, suggested that she had been wearing shoes for years. There were the smallest of cracks on her soles and you could eat porridge off the top of her feet. She also had these impossibly beautifully trimmed fingernails and she had the habit of placing her hands on the desk in front of her, back straight and eyes staring ahead of her. I immediately nicknamed her Sphinx and, although I meant it as a compliment, she cried when someone was tactless enough to call her that to her face. She carried her books in a store-bought canvas backpack. But Lorraine could neither read nor write. She could not tell the time. She sat in her assigned seat, never fooling around or whispering or tossing papers, like some angel out of place. I had nicknamed her Sphinx because of the way she extended her dainty hands in front of her, resting them on the desk. I thought she was beautiful.

The class did not know what to do with her. Each day she brought two slices of bread, glued together with some kind of paste, and called the stuck-together bread a sandwich. She ate her sandwich delicately from a pink plastic container and sipped a strange kind of soup or gravy from a little blue plastic bottle. After one term, she disappeared. Perhaps she went to Zambia, for it was rumoured that her father came from there. I was actually happy for Lorraine. She would never have survived Mrs Monyatsi. She had been skittish, fearful and not tough enough for Mrs Monyatsi.

I doubted my own survival chances, but still I was certain that Lorraine would have had no chances at all. Mrs Monyatsi's husband was a *sekopa*, a man completely under the thumb of his wife. There were few men like him and they were treated with contempt. Even a child sent by a *sekopa* would visibly drag his or her feet. Once we had come across Mr Monyatsi by the river and he called out to us and told us to go and get him a chicken at someone's house. With any other adult, we would have hidden our displeasure and complied. But with Mr Monyatsi, we simply pretended we did not understand what he was saying, until he gave up. His family had twice made him undergo a vomiting treatment, under the supervision of a very knowledgeable witchdoctor, but nothing had changed. He still cooked for their young children and it was rumoured that he had once been observed sweeping the family yard. The image of a man bending over, holding a grass broom, sweeping a yard, was too fantastic for me to imagine, so I never really believed that rumour. So, Mrs Monyatsi was not just a terror at school, she had a whole grown man dancing to her tune. We even half-believed the story that she did on occasion beat Mr Monyatsi. My grandmother said that, most probably, the witchdoctor who had rendered him a *sekopa* had died, otherwise he would have long taken pity on him and minimised the effects of his spells over Mr Monyatsi.

Another girl who left our school was Rose. She left after only two months into the term. But Mrs Monyatsi had nothing to do with Rose's leaving our school. In fact, Mrs Monyatsi would have loved for Rose to stay. Rose had never suffered any of Mrs Monyatsi's thrashing or taunts. Mrs Monyatsi was so shamelessly protective of Rose that it was embarrassing to everyone, including Rose. She would fuss over her and give her answers to questions. She praised her endlessly and made her stand up in front of the class for us to admire her neat uniform, her trimmed fingernails and her clean hair. We didn't play with Rose, not because we didn't like her, but because we were afraid to harm her in any way and then get into trouble with Mrs Monyatsi. What if you stepped on her during a skipping rope game? What if you threw dirt on her neat uniform during a *diketo* game? What if you hit her too hard during a dodge ball game? Rose didn't abuse her special status, but still, getting involved with her in any way would have been reckless in the extreme. What if I chewed on her rubber by mistake? The risks were too high, so we ignored her and excluded her.

Mrs Monyatsi interpreted our exclusion of Rose to mean that Rose was too much of a lady to play our games. 'Rose plays tennis with the missionaries' children. She has no need to play these dusty games of yours. Oh Rose, can't you teach them to be ladies, like you? And you speak English through your nose, like a real English lady! They will never ever come close to you!' Rose would smile with embarrassment and we would feel sorry for her because it was not her fault that Mrs Monyatsi was so pathetically trying to impress her. Rose had been born in England. I had not thought that it was possible for a black child to be born in England or a white child to be born in Mochudi. I had thought there was a law against it. All the missionary women disappeared from the village only to come back with toddlers, months later. But Rose had been born in England as surely as the sun came from the East – the evidence was all there, in the way she spoke and gestured and jutted her chin forward.

Rose was the daughter of a man, whom she called Papa, who dressed up in white clothes and played a game called tennis with the missionary doctors, ministers and other white men associated with the Deborah Retief Memorial Hospital and the Dutch Reformed Church. It was quite embarrassing to see a grown Motswana man behaving like a child – hitting a ball over a sagging net and running around like that. Rose's mother, whom she called Mama, was a quiet woman who kept to herself and refused to join the white wives as they watched their white-clad husbands playing tennis.

It was rumoured that Rose's father was very much into white ways and that he was moving the family from Mochudi to Gaborone so that Rose would have only English-speaking playmates.

Whatever the truth, Mrs Monyatsi was impressed by Rose's father's ways. Just before he decamped to Gaborone, he came to school to have a chat with Mrs Monyatsi about Rose's progress in school. If she had grovelled any lower, she would have been been strangled by tree roots, as my grandmother would have said. Afterwards she was flustered and sweaty and she even let us out of school early.

Rose's father had worked at the District Commissioner's office where he spoke English all day. Even though we didn't play with Rose, still we envied her and we imagined her in Gaborone, speaking English with a nasal accent, eating chicken and rice every day and swimming in crystal clear water. Mary said there was a big hole dug into the earth in Gaborone where white people, and people like Rose's father who were into white ways, could swim. We challenged her, because we could not imagine naked children and adults, cupping their private parts with left hand and pinching their noses with their right, jumping successively into a hole full of water and playing as if they were age mates. But Mary stuck to her story and swore that everyone took off their clothes and put on clingy little garments before going into the water. She was adamant that women as old as my grandmother got up to this nonsense. She said that the hole was not muddy as the walls had been protected with cement and painted blue. We didn't know whether to believe everything she said but we did suspect that white people, and people who were adopting white ways, were doing rather strange things in Gaborone. One of them, an aunt of Mary's actually was, we heard, learning how to drive a car! She was working for a Mr Walters as a housemaid, but this Mr Walters it seemed, had gotten it into his head that a black woman could drive a car and was teaching Mary's aunt. So it was possible, we conceded rather reluctantly, that there was a swimming hole in Gaborone. Whatever took place in Gaborone, Rose was a lucky girl, we reckoned. Soon she would completely forget how to speak Setswana and she would be on her path to success. And pleasant as she was, with her English mannerisms and her endless 'pleases and thank yous', we were happy that Rose was gone. Life could return to normal.

I wondered what the Missionaries would do with the three seats, close to the white section of the church, that had been reserved for Rose and her parents. Would the white church-goers spill into that section of the Church? Or would black people be allowed to sit there? My grandmother called this area 'the zebra section' and Mary's family 'the zebra family' and stated authoritatively that, as best she could remember, there had not been a zebra family in the Dutch Reformed Church for twenty years.

For me, though, attempting to drop out would have earned me a beating from my mother who had decided that she would do everything in her power to keep me in school. She might even have surrendered me to my father for the punishment. As a girl, to be thrashed by one's father was the ultimate punishment. It meant you were a *seganana,* that is, an incorrigible wayward child. I had never suffered such humiliation and I did not wish to. Also, dropping out would have brought the Principal and the Catholic Priest to come and find out why I was not in school. The Catholic Priest had taken it upon himself to badger people he hardly knew into returning their children to school. The Principal tagged along on the demand of the Catholic Priest. Just as bad, dropping out would have meant working in the fields. Even with the constant beatings, writing and reading and learning how to tell time were preferable to hauling water, hewing wood, picking beans and looking after goats, day in and day out. And, the school had started providing food to students during playtime. The Principal had renamed the break to mealtime. But we still did squeeze in some play into the break.

Renaming was big that year, or at least that is how it seemed to me. Our school was, for example, renamed Lady Locklear Primary School after a yellow-dressed woman alighted from an impressive automobile, floated over the sand towards us, as we waited in neat lines, and spoke fast and furiously in a language which must have been English. After she left, we were informed that she had donated money for sixty chairs to the Standard One classes and that we would be changing our name to honour her. But neither the new English name nor the chance to sit on a new chair alone would have been sufficient to entice me back to school.

There was yet another very good reason to stay in school. I had joined the school athletics team and a trip to Molepolole was scheduled for soon after term started. The only time I had ever left the village was to go to the cattle post and to the lands and then I had either walked or ridden in a donkey cart or a sled. I knew from other members of the team that the five-hour ninety-kilometre trip, in the back of an open government truck was something special to experience. The school would provide bread, canned pilchards, oranges and even Cool-aid for a lunch break at some point after Gaborone. The thought of missing such a sumptuous lunch made me concentrate on the fact that no one had actually died at Mrs Monyatsi's hands. There had been nasty nosebleeds and split lips here and there, and a broken arm once, but no one had actually been buried. And I had never ridden in a motor vehicle and Mrs

23

Monyatsi was not about to deny me a space in the green Bedford truck. There was also the possibility, although a bit remote, that I would be photographed. My classmate Mary, who was in the school netball team, had been photographed while on a trip to Serowe. She actually had a picture of herself stuck to the inside of her science exercise book.

So I stayed in school and tried to do as little as possible to get Mrs Monyatsi's attention. I did all my homework, promptly divided any new pencil into four equal pieces and gave the other three to my grandmother for safe-keeping. My mother has stopped doing that for me, expecting that I was too old to be losing pencils like a Sub A or Sub B pupil, but I was not going to take chances with Mrs Monyatsi. Showing up without a pencil or having lost a book was perhaps the biggest offence. These offences attracted very harsh penalties, including expulsion from the class and denial of food.

I polished my shoes as best I could, even if most times I had to use lard to get a hint of a shine, and ensured that I did not lose buttons from my school uniform. I washed as well as I could with the limited facilities at home. I particularly washed my face, arms and legs, the parts that would be visible to Mrs Monyatsi. I soaked my cracked feet and hands in water and rubbed them all over with a rough stone to reduce the crevices. Occasionally, there was a bit of Vaseline to oil my constantly dry skin.

On weekends I ground up charcoal and brushed my teeth as best I could with the powder and a bit of water. And I continued to thank the Lord Jesus for keeping the story of one of my great-great-grandmothers from Mrs Monyatsi.

The story, which even in my family was whispered only very rarely, was that one of my great-great-grandmothers had been found in the company of a married man under circumstances that suggested an amorous relationship. The story was that perhaps the large nose that had since made its appearance on the faces of some of my family members was due to that particular link. As the story went, a cow had been paid at the time and none of the marriages, for my great-great-grandmother had been married too, were broken as a result. It was an old story and its truth was even questionable, still such rumours were better kept away from Mrs Monyatsi for she could rattle a skeleton louder than anyone I had ever known. No one had the courage to point out to her face that she had bewitched her own husband, who as a result cooked, rode around on an old mule, muttering foolishly and wore a permanent grin.

'Child of Motlatsi, who in turn was child of Mosung who was divorced for witchcraft, and was sent home riding on a thorn bush, what did you eat this morning?' she bellowed at Nina barely ten days into the new year. Mrs Monyatsi's face reminded me of a dog in our neighbourhood. The sly eyes, too close to each other, the long face. It wasn't really an ugly face, but it was frightening. In fact, she had a sister who looked almost exactly like her and she was an attractive women. But when Mrs Monyatsi got really worked up, her face got contorted and I thought saliva would surely start dripping down the corners of her mouth.

'*Motogo* Mistress,' was the whispered reply. Everybody knew that teachers had eggs and liver and bread for breakfast. Not that any of us had seen a teacher eating, but still what else could a teacher eat? Teachers lived in 'teachers' quarters' comprising square-shaped houses painted a pale yellow. They had a communal tap from which they fetched water pumped there from a borehole situated just outside the school compound. Teachers used pit-latrines while almost everybody else used the bushes next to the river as toilets. So teachers did not have *motogo* for breakfast, or at least that was what we all thought.

'Child of Motlatsi, who in turn was child of Mosung who was divorced for witchcraft, and was sent home riding on a thorn bush, what kind of soap did you use this morning?'

'Pig soap, Mistress.'

'Child of Motlatsi, who in turn was child of Mosung who was divorced for witchcraft, and was sent home riding on a thorn bush, I said what kind of soap did you use this morning?' Mrs Monyatsi's voice had risen to a dangerous level and I was trying to sit as still as possible, lest she suddenly decided on attacking me.

'Pig soap, Mistress.'

'Louder!'

'Pig soap!'

'Pig soap what, child of Motlatsi?'

'Pig soap, Mistress!'

'Yes, I knew there was a filthy pig in this classroom. You are all pigs and you all smell like pigs. Out you go. Round the block. Sing out loud: 'We are pigs, we smell. We are pigs, we smell.'

We all trooped out and shouted, abusing ourselves for all to hear. Every time we passed our classroom we all put extra verve in our self-humiliation. Child of Motlatsi did not come back when school reopened for the second term. In fact Nina, child of Motlatsi, married a gold-miner and proceeded to have one child every two years and within a couple of years one could have been excused for mistaking her for Motlatsi, her mother – this on account of her ill-fitting clothes, headscarf and snuff-snorting. Life in school had been hard but life out of school turned out to be brutal. I decided to stay in school and to take my chances with Mrs Monyatsi.

As for Mrs Monyatsi, she broke rather foul-smelling wind and blamed it on the class. I could always tell even before the smell reached the second row, where I sat, sharing a desk with Mary. Mrs Monyatsi would tilt her bottom slightly, to give the air a chance to escape without making a sound. The situation was particularly bad in the afternoon after lunch, when the classroom was hot and the air was still.

'Go out and shake your smelly disgusting selves!' she would bark. We would leap off our chairs and file out. Being slow and showing anything close to a lack of enthusiasm could earn the offender a Ninety Degrees.

'Ninety Degrees' was what Mrs Monyatsi called bending over at a ninety-degree angle, without touching your ankles, and receiving nine strokes from a cane. Ninety-Degrees was to be particularly avoided because Mrs Monyatsi did not allow 'degree shifts' as she called any movements resulting in any deviation from the prescribed angle. Thus any movement from a pupil who is receiving Ninety Degrees would lead the punishment starting all over again.

'Boys and girls, did I see a degree shift?' She would bellow.

'You did, Mistress!' The chorus was always loud and energetic. Mrs Monyatsi's swivelling eyes could detect an unenthusiastic response.

'Boys and girls, what should I not see?'

'A degree shift, Mistress!'

'Boys and girls, what should I see?'

'Ninety degrees, Mistress!'

So as soon as Mrs Monyatsi did her surreptitious tilt, I prepared myself for the inevitable scramble through the door. Once outside I would shake my dress, as would all the other girls. The boys would pound their pants and stomp their feet. We would all hop about until the Mrs Monyatsi called us back into the classroom. When we got back into the classroom, we were at great pains not to wrinkle our noses in response to the still foul air. Faces would be blank, with noses in place. The efforts of keeping a straight face would have been comical, were it not for the seriousness of the situation.

'Now sit down and finish your compositions. Remember the topic, "The Happiest Day of My Life".' There was a well-known story of a not-too-bright student years before, who, faced with the same topic, had written about how he expected his last day in Standard One to be the happiest day of his life. The composition had earned him three ninety degrees and a zero decorated with eyes and a tail. A decorated zero was to be avoided as it earned one a special visit to the Principal's office for further caning. So each one of us, without consultations or even thinking that there could possibly be any other story to tell, cited the first day of our Standard One school year as the happiest day of our lives. Another of Mrs Monyatsi's favourite topics was, 'What I like about my Teacher'. Mrs Monyatsi produced quick studies, so that Berka Solomon, who joined our class mid-term from another school, was able to produce a glowing description of Mrs Monyatsi within a week of joining our class. 'Mrs Monyatsi is kind and good teacher,' Berka Solomon had written. 'She like clean pupils and she like pupils who listen good good. She like students that are respect teachers well well and write homework neat neat and clean clean in lines. She don't like children who rub books with finger and maker holes in book. Mrs Monyatsi is best teacher in hole world. Mrs Monyatsi is teacher I like very very much. Mrs Monyatsi is good teacher very much.' Mrs Monyatsi read out Berka Solomon's composition to the class. Berka Solomon beamed with pride, especially when he was sent to the Principal's office to collect his white ribbon. I had worn the white ribbon a few times myself but, as much as it was coveted, there was a downside. To return it, brown and soiled, at the end of the day could earn one a beating from the Principal. The result was that any sensible white-ribbon-wearer had to refrain from playing, for there was no way one could be part of any type of play without coming into contact with the bright red earth. The result, though, was that a white-ribbon-wearer appeared to the rest of the class to be showing off, sitting quietly, watching others play, donning the impossible-to-miss ribbon. White-ribbon-wearing did not earn the wearer friends.

Often I felt like I lived two sets of lives, the school life and the home life. The home life itself was divided into two, that is the village life and the lands life. It did not help that we moved between village, lands and cattle post, depending on the season and whether school was on or off. It also did not help that my siblings never seemed to be together in any one place. There was, I felt, a constant shifting and restlessness, and what I learned at school did not seem to have any real-life application. Then there were the unreasonable rules that were based solely on whether you were in school or at home. For example, I wished I could wear my school shoes at home, especially at the lands. After having two years of stuffing paper inside the shoes to fill in the two-sizes-too-large space, the shoes were finally a perfect fit. They had been bought two sizes too big so they could last me longer, which made sense because I had no younger school-going sibling to pass them on to and no older school-going sibling to take over used shoes from. But, with my well-fitting sturdy shoes, I would have been able to run into the bush, confident that I was protected from thorns, millipedes, snakes and scorpions. My brother Leruo had sent me a comfortable, sturdy pair of shoes but I could not wear them to the lands. I had never understood why the shoes were reserved for school, church and the hospital only. Those were three places without thorns, millipedes, snakes or scorpions. In fact, the church steps felt nice and cool on my bare feet. But that was how things were. Just like in the matter of chairs. At school, at church and at the hospital, it was okay for children and women to sit on chairs or benches. But it was not okay to do so at home. At home only men sat on chairs. That was just the way it was. Even though there was the problem of doing homework. It was so much easier to write homework while sitting on a chair, with the books resting on a table. But I could not dare do that. So I did my homework lying down on my tummy or sitting cross-legged on the floor with my book resting on my left hand. Sometimes, I used a flat-topped rock that was under a tree in our yard, to rest my exercise book. But I would only use the rock during the day and when the shade was right, because it was too heavy to move about in the yard. Another puzzle was why, when your mother tried to beat you, running to hide behind another adult ended the matter right there, but one could not do the same at school. At home, it was considered a way of apology and an act showing respect for both adults but, at school, it was considered disrespectful and could earn you additional lashes. There were clearly things that belonged to four cornered houses and things that belonged to round houses. Keeping them straight was not always easy.

CHAPTER 3

M y mother was a quiet, perhaps shy woman. Even when she was shouting at us there was a muted quality to her voice. Members of the extended family consulted her on all kinds of matters. Aunts openly came to ask her to talk to their daughters and uncles consulted her on male topics, while pretending to indulge her in her need for gossip. She would give her advice in a quiet measured way, guiding the person seeking advice to a solution without seeming opinionated. There was, for example, the time when Rra-Bina came over to our yard, just minutes after my father had left for the cattle post. Immediately I tended the fire for tea, for I knew how he loved tea. It was always best to start an errand before being asked, especially as I was, at the time, hoping for a new dress for Christmas.

Rra-Bina skirted around the topic that had brought him to our yard but finally he started, 'Mma-Leruo, I have come to ask for your advice. My son, Bina, is top of his class and I fear that too much of the white man's knowledge might render him insane.'

Indeed that was a concern of many parents. Cramming too much information, especially information on mathematics and science, into a child's head could make them go mad. My aunts and uncles had warned me many times about not reading all the time.

'You are a lucky man, Rra-Bina, your son Bina will become a teacher or perhaps even an Agricultural Demonstrator. You should be happy that he is so smart.'

'But what if he goes mad with all this stuff they are forcing into his head? Surely there is that danger, Mma-Monei.'

'Do you know anyone who had suffered this fate? Me, I don't. But maybe I know too little of these matters.'

'There is Mogotsi, the son of Morobi, who went to Tiger Kloof, then to London and now he is mad! He was a fine young man, until he read and wrote like a white man. Now look at him. What is the use of education if all you do is go around muttering in English!'

'But his grandfather was mad too, wasn't he? But he never went to school. What can we blame for his madness?'

'Are you saying then, that too much education is not bad for the children?'

'What I'm saying is that white men get educated and do not go mad. Why should black people go mad when they learn the same thing?'

'Well, I can't say that we have the same kind of brains, Mma-Monei. Surely we don't? And these things the children are learning, they are English things. They are strange things. They don't learn about things you and I see and can touch. I'm really thinking of taking Bina out of school, so he can herd cattle at the cattle post. He doesn't want to leave school and that meddlesome Father James is on my back about it. That squinting man is a pain, if you ask me. Can't a man make decisions about his family without having to worry about some churchman badgering him? Have I ever told him how to run his church?'

'Let's leave Father James out of this for a while, Rra-Bina. Your son is very smart. He could, one day, become a Principal of a school. He could even work for the District Commissioner. Or he could work as an officer in an office in Gaborone. What about a police officer? Don't you have dreams of him wearing a suit and carrying a notebook and investigating crime? Writing down important matters? I don't believe that school can make children mad. That is just talk. Let him stay in school. You will not regret it.' The two had discussed the matter back and forth and Rra-Bina had finally decided to keep his son in school, at least for the time being.

My mother was also a herbalist for babies and new mothers. She knew roots, berries, leaves and barks that could cure all kinds of ailments associated with childbirth. New mothers came to her to consult about bleedings that would not stop as well as to firm up a baby's collapsed fontanel. This kept her very busy and, of all of us, only my sister Mmadira seemed keen to learn my mother's trade. Noka, being a boy, was the one often sent to dig the roots or bring some bark or berry home, but he was not interested in learning their particular uses. Mmadira would be the one to examine and prepare the herbs.

It was a trade because she charged a fee for her services. Still, she could not turn those without a chicken away, for that was her standard fee anyway. The ancestors would have taken her gift away, had she used it only to enrich herself. My mother was therefore a very busy woman, for the village was full of babies and mothers requiring her skills. I think there were times when I was resentful. But most times, I was very proud of my mother's seemingly extensive knowledge. She came from a family of healers. But never bone casters. That was good because those who cast bones to divine the ills and fortunes of others were often witches as well. And if not actually witches, they had the potential anyway. My mother's father had been a *thobega* doctor, a setter of broken bones. A good bonesetter, and my grandfather, from all accounts, was very good and commanded respect. It was expected that one of us children would inherit the art of healing and Mmadira had indeed demonstrated that she was the chosen one. The art of healing was not just a blessing, but it was a major responsibility as well. A chosen one could not just decide to ignore the calling, for she or he would, as a result, be plagued by ill health and emotional restlessness. My sister Mmadira seemed keen on the trade she had inherited so my parents were very much relieved. My mother told her friends with utter admiration, that Mmadira had had a good eye and nose for herbs since she was ten years old.

My sister Mmadira earned my everlasting respect and awe after the day she brought my classmate Mary back from the clutches of death. My mother was not home when Mary was brought to our house by her distraught parents. She was limp and her eyes seemed to be rolling around on their own. She had obviously been vomiting. Mmadira took one look at her and in minutes she had a concoction for her to drink. She couldn't drink unaided so Mmadira forced the liquid down her throat. Mmadira was not that much bigger than her patient but she acted authoritatively and efficiently. She announced that from the smell of the vomit Mary had eaten *molefe,* a beetle we knew to be extremely poisonous but which was visually similar to *lebere,* an edible beetle. Having caused Mary to ingest a cupful of a herbal concoction, she screamed across the *lapa* wall, for a breastfeeding neighbour to come over. Once the neighbour presented herself, Mmadira demanded that she express some milk into a cup and within minutes Mary was being force-fed the milk. For two full hours, Mmadira fed Mary breast milk and the herbal concoction alternately and for that whole period Mary seemed to vomit continuously. Finally, Mmadira fed her something that seemed to make her sleep. By the time my mother came, Mary was stirring and asking in a weak voice for her mother. Mmadira had been only sixteen or seventeen when she saved Mary's life.

My mother was so proud of Mmadira's prompt and efficient response that she organised a ceremony at which she invited other healers for Mmadira's special recognition.

CHAPTER 4

L ife at the lands, which I was part of on weekends and on
school holidays, was so far removed from life at the village
that it often seemed to me that the people changed as well. They
walked and talked differently, I thought. The neatly thatched
rondavels with the gaily decorated walls of the village compounds
were nowhere to be seen at the lands. Instead, the compounds
comprised of huts thatched with less regard to aesthetics. Further,
the compound perimeter fence was thorn bushes while at the
village there were sturdy decorated walls. The lands compounds
seemed to melt into the bushy surroundings while the village ones
seemed to be designed to stand out.

I was walking to the well to fetch water and to water the goats
one school holiday in the company of my sister Keneilwe and my
sister Mmadira. Keneilwe was the undisputed champion of footprint watching and interpretation. Everybody said it was because
she was nosy that she spent so much time watching the sandy path
to find out who went where, when and especially with whom. She
was walking ahead of us and keeping to the shoulder of the path.

'Oh, I see, Mosidi has new shoes. My, that's interesting. Perhaps her man has arrived from the mines. Interesting I hadn't
heard that he was coming. She is going to have to wean that two-
year-old child of hers.' Keneilwe nodded speculatively as she
walked along.

'Maybe she bought the shoes after selling that bag of beans she
was talking about the other day,' suggested Mmadira.

'No, I don't think so. She needed that money for food for her
school children. I don't see her buying shoes when the children are

starving. And her youngest needed a school sweater. She didn't have enough to buy that! No, her man must have arrived with money from the mines.'

We came to a fork on the path and immediately Keneilwe exclaimed, 'And who was Tebogo walking with? And look they were walking side-by-side. Could be they were even holding hands! Look at the distance between these sets of prints! Who is this? Someone new, I dare say! These aren't Senatla's prints. I wonder what he would say if he found out!'

'You don't think that's her husband? You don't think that those are Senatla's shoe prints?'

'No way that's her husband!' Keneilewe was almost hopping with excitement. 'Look at that left foot! It twists as it lifts. And those feet are smaller than Senatla's. That's interesting. Perhaps I will pay Tebogo a visit later today. Oh, I see there is a child I don't know walking around with Mma-Saebo's children. Perhaps a nephew who's come to visit.'

'Do you have to be so inquisitive?' Mmadira was shaking her head at her cousin. 'You really want to know everything that takes place! Remember, a duiker with a long neck gets killed by arrows not meant for it!'

Keneilwe just shook her head and smiled. 'You too are interested. I see that poor Kabusu is still walking bare foot! There is a lazy man! Won't make himself the poorest pair of sandals! My father even offered him pieces of cowhide last week. I bet it's rotting somewhere as we speak. And look! Supang's goats have just been let out of the kraal! That man he has hired to herd his goats is useless! I must inform Supang next time I go to Mochudi. Perhaps I will go to Mochudi tomorrow after we finish stamping the sorghum. His goats will die from hunger if this herdsman keeps on starving them like this. You can see they were running to the well for water. They must have been thirsty. Yes, I must tell Supang.'

'And why are you so sure they were let out late? And aren't you just looking for an excuse to see Supang?' There was a suggestive twinkle in Mmadira's eye.

'What do you mean? I have no interest in Supang, other than the fact that he is a lonely man with no children and a useless goatherd. The poor man is still mourning his wife. I would never have improper thoughts about a man in mourning. And, of course the goats have just been let out. Look at how their prints have trampled all the other prints. I know Selinah left for Mochudi a little while ago. I saw her pass by but I do not see her footprints anywhere here. Must have been trampled by the goat. Means only one thing to me.'

Bored with the footprint watching and interpretations by my older sister, I suggested that I go join Noka and help him herd the goats to the well. I knew that Noka was in the bushes somewhere driving the goats towards the well for their daily drink. At first Keneilwe was reluctant to let me go into the thick bush by myself.

'Then whistle for Noka. He will come and get me,' I suggested.

'I told you to learn to whistle,' my sister admonished. 'How can you hope to be effective at goat-herding when you cannot acquire the most basic of herding skills!'

'Well, I am not drinking a bull's urine, even if it means I never learn how to whistle!' I protested hotly.

'Well then, let's see how you survive in this bush without being able to whistle!' I had been repeatedly told I would have to drink the urine of a bull if I wanted to learn how to whistle. I had watched as my siblings and my cousins had gladly cupped warm urine from under the family bull but I had had no desire to join in the fun. The whistling seemed to come after many days of constant practice but that the bull's urine was the catalyst was in no doubt. I was the only one who could not whistle.

'Stop talking to this poor child as if you are talking to some cattle-post boy! If she can't whistle, she can't! Leave her alone. After all, she is attending school. She doesn't need to know how to herd goats. She is going to be a teacher. Or perhaps a nurse. We don't need a whistling nurse now, do we?' That I was going to be either a teacher or a nurse had been said so many times, by almost every member of the family, that I was beginning to wonder whether I had any choice in the matter.

Keneilwe whistled and within seconds a response was heard from Noka. After a few back and forth whistles, Noka appeared from the bushes and I joined him.

Within half an hour Noka and I were sitting by the well, waiting for the goats to finish drinking. Keneilwe and Mmadira left with strict orders that we ensure that the goats keep away from the fields.

More children came and soon the well area was abuzz. Most of the boys made clay cows for toys while the girls skipped rope. Then Oupa, who had been playing and talking civilly, seemed to remember that he had unfinished business with me. I was busy swinging my end of the rope when I realised that all eyes were directed at a spot behind me. I turned, to see Oupa's extended right arm and in his palm was some sand. I knew immediately that I was being challenged to a fight. I had two choices. To walk away, and be declared a coward, or to slap the hand down as a sign of accepting the challenge. I could not remember crossing Oupa so I was not sure why I was being challenged. I let go of my end of the rope and slapped Oupa's hand down and then punched him in the stomach. As he doubled over, muttering that I had sneaked in a punch before he was ready, Noka stepped forward. 'You can't fight a girl. I will stand in for my sister. Boys fight boys and girls fight girls. Those are the rules!'

'But you are older than Oupa,' someone piped in. 'That would be unfair.'

'Okay then, I will stand in for my sister,' my cousin Thapelo, who was the same age as Oupa, declared as he stepped forward.

'Why are you challenging me, anyways?' I wanted to know, still watchful and ready to throw another punch, in case he came after me.

'You called me guitar chest when I was sick and thin last year.'

'I did not!'

'Yes you did.'

'I did not!'

'Yes you did. Minki told me.'

'Minki, the story spinner? She lied to you! Why would you believe Minki? She lies all the time!'

'It's too late now. You accepted his challenge. You can't back down now!' Simon loved a good fight and he was not about to let the matter be resolved amicably. He waved his hands to indicate that the two fighters should be given space. But tempers had cooled and unless someone thought of some other reason to stoke the moment, there was not going to be any fight.

'What about you, Simon?' someone chipped in. 'You insulted Oupa during the ploughing season. You said his knees were like those of an ostrich.'

Simon was not a fighter but rather a moderator at fights. He was thus relieved to hear, as Oupa approached him with balled fists, an older voice bellow above the chatter, 'Break it up! You are supposed to be watching the goats not fighting. All of you go check on your goats.' At this, we disappeared into the bushes to find and herd our respective goats from the direction of the fields. The man who had spoken was Rra-Minki but we had all responded because an adult had spoken.

'I would have knocked that silly boy down if you people had let me.' I broke the silence once we were a safe distance from Rra-Minki. 'I never said his chest looked like a guitar and Minki had no business lying about me. Maybe I should knock her crooked teeth in for that!'

'Yes, but you should not fight boys you know. It's not right. Boys must fight boys and girls must fight girls!'

'But you fight me all the time.'

'That's different. We are brother and sister. And you should not fight me anyway. I am your older brother. You must call me Abuti Noka and respect me!'

'Do you want to fight about it? Is that it? Your fists are itching?' I had stopped to face him.

'Forget about it. I am not fighting you and getting myself a thrashing from Rra-Minki. He told us to stop and we must stop. And Mma-Leruo has said many times that we should stop fighting. You just want to get us into trouble with this fighting talk of yours.'

'Okay then, I will race you to Old Man Toto's field. To the Morula tree at the Western entrance! You take the right route and I will take the left route. No cheating and no going through any fields.'

'Okay with me. Three claps and we go.'

A few minutes later we met, huffing and puffing, at the designated place. We agreed that there was no winner and no loser.

Noka however had not given up on a matter he had raised earlier on. 'Monei, will you please promise to call me Abuti Noka tomorrow at the well? Please? I want my friends to know that I am respected.' I remained quiet for a while considering what I could ask for in return but my brother continued, 'If you do, then I will give you my two eggs on the *mosu* tree. The ones I found yesterday on our way to the salt pan.'

I could not believe that my brother would offer such a valuable find. I looked up and when I realised that my brother was serious it dawned on me how much he wanted to play the big brother before our cousins and friends. My heart softened and I promised, 'All right, I promise to call you Abuti Noka for the whole year. Until Christmas. But you have to promise to be nice to me too. You can't tell me to go away whenever you are with your friends.'

'But I am giving you two eggs! They will hatch soon and you can have them all by yourself! I will not ask for a piece! I promise I won't! You can't say I must play with you all the time! Other boys are already laughing at me. They say I am always touching *makgabe*. That I will never shoot straight!'

'Okay then, I will call you Abuti Noka and you give me the two eggs. I roast the birds and eat them by myself. Maybe I will give you a small piece. But I don't play with you when your friends are around but when they are not around I can play with you.' I extended my pinky to seal the deal and my brother did likewise. When our fingers were linked I sliced them apart with my left hand.

'Should we swear by the fontanel of a baby?' Noka asked.

'No,' I answered firmly.

'I guess you are right.' There was too much uncertainty about our bargain to risk the health of a baby. The eggs may not hatch or if they hatch the birds may fly away before capture. A snake might eat the eggs. I might forget and call Noka without the honorific 'Abuti'. Still, we meant to keep our respective ends of the bargain.

'Monei, will you take yesterday's thorn from my foot. It should be ripe and easy today. Maybe I would have beat you in the race if it wasn't for the thorn.'

'Maybe, maybe not! But yes. I will take it out. Let me have your foot.'

Indeed, within minutes, I had gently dug out the thorn from Noka's foot. I had tried the previous day, but Noka had not been able to stand the pain, so I had plugged the entry point of the thorn with earwax. The result was that, within forty-eight hours, the area around the thorn was slightly septic, making it easier to squeeze the thorn out.

Soon it was time to herd the goats closer to the homestead so we could have our midday meal.

'What do you think Ausi Keneilwe is cooking for lunch?' Noka asked.

'Ausi Keneilwe said she was going to kill the old rooster. It's been useless now for a while. So into the pot it goes!' I was indeed hoping we would be having chicken stew for lunch. Keneilwe would no doubt give the intestines to Noka and I so we could boil them and make extra sauce for ourselves. The thought alone was enough to get my stomach grumbling.

'Is that why you took Botlhe to aunt Mma-Lesego's compound this morning?' Botlhe, our niece, simply refused to eat meat from an animal if she had seen it being slaughtered. Schemes were always being devised to remove her from the scene, because just knowing that an animal was going to be slaughtered was enough to set her off crying and begging for its life.

'Yes. And now that you mention her, I have to pick her up before we go home. Can you walk me there, please? I don't like walking alone in the bush. We can drive the goats that way and leave them at the Sesu Pan for the afternoon.'

'I will, as long as you promise to help me separate the goats from the kids when you get home. And I promise to help you do the dishes tonight. And let's hope we don't get sent to chase the birds off the field tomorrow. I hope we get sent to collect firewood instead!'

'I agree with you there. That ridiculously short sorghum the government is promoting is a problem.' For the second year in a row, the government, whoever the government was, for I was becoming confused on that point, had given out free sorghum seeds for planting. The new sorghum was of a supposedly superior variety to the local one because the plant did not grow as tall – and therefore matured quicker – and it had bigger kernels. The problem was that, because the plant was so short, we did not just have to worry about weaverbirds eating the sorghum, we had to worry about doves as well. The traditional variety, being taller and thinner, would have been too wobbly for doves to land on. As if that were not enough, my mother complained that harvesting the short, government-promoted sorghum killed her back. Instead of bending the stalk to her level, as she would have done with the traditional sorghum, she had to bend to the stunted government sorghum. 'With the amount of kernels I lost to the doves, I get less than half the usual harvest. And to top it all, I get a ruined back! What's the use of bigger kernels of sorghum, if the doves take them from under your nose? I hope this is not the way of this new government. Next time they will be telling us they can make rain! You watch! You are there, I am here, they will be claiming that! Haven't they already claimed they will build us bridges, rivers and roads?' Both my parents were very skeptical about the claims made by the new government. The Queen, they argued, had promised very little and delivered even less. They were also unhappy about the rumour that a bicycle tax was being contemplated. 'We plunge through the bush, making paths for our bicycles, and now they want to tax us? Will they make bicycle roads to lands and cattle posts? Next thing you know they will be demanding feet tax!' my father fumed. My father didn't have a bicycle, but that didn't stop him from having a strong opinion on the matter. Noka and I had heard about the hut tax levied by the Queen and, as far as we knew, the Queen hadn't had to help with building the hut, so the arguments against the bicycle tax didn't quite make sense. But then tax didn't make sense either.

'Will you help me with Tibe tomorrow?' Noka asked with begging eyes.

'No way! I'm certainly not helping you with that!' Tibe was the family cat and it had been decided that it needed castration. Not only was castration a boy's task, but I was not about to help hold down a furious cat while someone sliced out its testicles with a knife! Noka would have to ask Thapelo or some other male cousin to help. He knew better than to ask me to help on something like that. Noka was always trying to get me to help him on boy's tasks, like the time he tried to convince me that nothing would happen to me if I helped him to clean up after Kimberly, his dog. Kimberly had always been good about going out of the yard until it was sprayed by a cobra. Not only was it nearly blinded, but it became timid and listless and would go anywhere in the yard. One of my tasks was to sweep the yard and Noka had tried to convince me that I could just sweep up the dog droppings with everything else. I wasn't about to risk being soft in the head, especially as we had just started a new math topic at school so I put my foot down. Dog pooh cleaning was a boy's job and that was that.

'But I gave you goat testicles last month. You didn't say no to that, did you now?' He was right. I had accepted his surreptitious offerings after my father had castrated the goats. They had actually been tasteless, especially since there was a taboo against salting them, and I hadn't understood the excitement among the boys. Girls were not supposed eat testicles but Noka had given me some.

'Yes, but it was just to taste. And I don't think our father would allow me to help with castrating the cat. Just ask him, if you think I'm being unfair.' We both agreed that I was right. In any case, neither of us wanted our father to find out about my eating the goat testicles. We just might be blamed for the still birth suffered by Sanko, a goat that for years had been dutifully producing two healthy goats every year. To mollify my brother somewhat, I promised to help him bag Tibe to take him to the field. The castration of the cat would have to be done at the field, so that it could run home afterwards. If it were castrated at the compound, it would run away for good.

CHAPTER 5

It was Monday morning, a day routinely used by teachers to find out about the personal details of their charges, under the innocent sounding title 'What I did over the weekend'. But this Monday, Mrs Moloi, our Standard Three teacher, wanted to know what each one of us wanted to be when we grew up. It was a question that had been asked many times before. Every teacher asked it and the responses hardly ever changed. Half the girls said they wanted to be teachers and most of the other half said they wanted to be nurses. Maureen wanted to be an air stewardess. This was because one of our books had a picture of a beautiful white girl, with long flowing hair, serving drinks to men in an airplane. And Mary wanted to be a bank-teller. There was a van that came into the village every month with big letters saying 'Mobile Bank' and the woman who gave out the salaries to the teachers called herself a bank-teller. She told the teachers what the bank had taken as charges for holding their money for them and what the government had withheld in tax. That was why she was a bank-teller. Or at least that was the explanation Mary gave. I didn't think I wanted to do that kind of job. Bank-telling seemed rather boring and, in any case, there didn't seem to be lots of job openings in bank-telling. I didn't find the uniform particularly impressive either and the repaired collar suggested that the job was not well paying. Some of the boys wanted to be school principals. There was clearly going to be a problem because they couldn't all become school principals, otherwise who would do the teaching? A couple of them said they want to be pilots. This was also on account of the book with the beautiful stewardess. It also had a picture of a handsome young man at the controls of an airplane. It was my turn and the class was waiting for my reply.

'Monei, are you with us? What do you want to be when you grow up?' I had stood up as was the custom when answering a question or making any contribution in class, but I had not said anything. There was impatience in Mrs Moloi's voice, but then I was one of her star pupils so she was not threatening to cane me. Yet.

'The Queen,' I blurted out. The class burst into laughter and Mrs Moloi frowned, then she laughed as well. I wanted to swallow back the answer but it was too late. 'You want to be the Queen? As in the Queen of England?' Mrs Moloi finally asked. She was trying to puzzle some sense out of the answer. She slipped her thick bottom lip into her mouth, as she always did when she was waiting for a response to an important question. I hung my head embarrassed but did not answer.

Mrs Moloi let her pink wet lip slip out of her mouth and regarded me thoughtfully, but still with some amusement, and declared, 'Well, you are not going to be the Queen of England, so can you come up with a more realistic ambition?' The class erupted again.

I wanted to explain but instead tears of humiliation sprang to my eyes. What I meant was that I wanted to make decisions like whether or not pupils should learn inches or centimetres. If I were the Queen, I would have allowed pupils all over the British Bechuanaland Protectorate to continue to use inches. Especially since some of them had just figured out that there are three feet in a yard and there are one thousand seven hundred and sixty yards in a mile. It did not seem right that the Queen would just decide that distance should be measured in centimetres, metres and kilometres just as I had come to grips with inches, feet and yards. But there was no time to explain. There were still ripples of laughter and I had to think of an answer quickly!

First I had thought I wanted to be a doctor but I knew that, as a girl, I could be a nurse only, not a doctor. I had seen only two doctors in my life and they had both been men and white. And I knew at least four girls called Nurse and three boys called Doctor. Nurse was a girl's name and Doctor was a boy's name. But the

Queen was a woman so I thought I had a chance there. Of course, there was talk of our country being independent from the Queen of England and a president going to take over. I could not say I wanted to be a president though because only men became presidents. And not just any men, but men who had been chiefs before or were at least related to one. That was why I wanted to be a queen. It had all seemed to make sense as I had worked it out in my mind while trying to learn how to whistle without drinking a bull's urine. But within the four white walls of my classroom, my classmates and my teacher were not seeing things my way. Clearly I had said something ridiculous.

'When I grow up, I want to be a teacher,' I whispered, still burning under the humiliation brought on by my quick answer. I made a mental note to learn to think before saying exactly what was in my head. Just as I must learn not to amaze my classmates and my teacher. It seemed like I was always doing both. Only the week before, we were given a poem to learn by heart and the following day I was able to recite it from start to finish without a stutter or a stumble. How could I stop the poem lodging itself in my brain? And once it was lodged in there, how could I stop it from tumbling flawlessly out?

'Good girl,' Mrs Moloi praised me on my revised professional plans. 'You will make an excellent teacher. You are a smart girl indeed. In fact, the boys in this class must be ashamed at being beaten by a girl in all tests!' The boys hung their heads and I tried to smile in triumph. But I wanted to tell her that I did not want to be a teacher because I had no intention of hitting young children. I could not imagine standing over small children waving a threatening cane, but I could not see how one could be a teacher without doing exactly that. Every time I declared that I wanted to be a teacher I spent the rest of the day worried that I would actually end up one. I was not too certain how teachers were made. I knew they went to a college in a far away village called Tonota to be taught how to teach. How to beat had to be part of the training as well, although I had to admit that each one of them had a unique way suited to his or her own character and temperament. Some pinched while others struck with objects. The objects varied from sticks and rulers to dusters. Some gave painless taps while others drew blood. Some smiled as they meted out punishment while others frowned with concentration. Some sweated while others did it effortlessly.

Sometimes, Mrs Moloi wrote the student's answers in a book and I was worried that I might be forced to become a teacher when the Queen or the President later consulted the book about our choices. If I became a teacher, I would have to decide on a method of punishment for my charges. I thought I would be amongst the frowners. I knew I could not be a principal because only men became principals. Although there was a story doing the rounds that Morwa South Primary School would be getting a female principal. I was not clear how this could possibly be so. But then, the woman came from Zululand and women from those parts were tall and strong as men. So perhaps a woman from Zululand could possibly be a principal.

Martha, squinting Martha who sat in the front row because she could not see the letters on the board otherwise, had, in her usual quiet voice, announced that she wanted to be a barrister. I had expected a titter from the class and a frown from Mrs Moloi, but there was only uncomfortable silence until Mrs Moloi went on to another pupil. It was clear that neither the teacher nor any of us knew what a barrister was. The word sounded authentic enough so no one dared laugh, lest she or he be proved to be the ignorant one. When I asked Martha later what a barrister was, she could only say that barristers were mentioned in a BBC World Service Report at 8 o'clock. The radio announcer had said, 'This is BBC World Service and the time is 8 o'clock. Three barristers from London ...' Martha had not been able to follow the rest of the report, on account of the announcer's very superior English accent, but Martha had figured out that barristers were important enough to be mentioned on BBC World Service. I was rather impressed for I had never been able to understand beyond, 'This is BBC World Service and the time is 8 o'clock.' In fact, that was always an indicator that the radio should be shut off to preserve the batteries. Between the two of us, we tentatively agreed that a barrister was most probably a woman who sat on a high stool writing out papers, putting an official stamp on some and a spike through the others. We arrived at this idea after considering quite a bit of information available to us and, of course, using our impressive brains. We knew that a bar-stool was a high chair used in important offices in Gaborone. We had never seen such a chair but we were pretty sure it existed. We also knew that a barrister had to be a woman because the 'ister' in barrister was clearly from the word 'sister'. We reasoned that a sister who sat on a high chair had to be very important. Important meant an office, papers, a red office stamp and a spike nearby. Thus 'barrister' was a profession worth aspiring to. We were not top of the class for nothing, Martha and I. I began to think that perhaps I wanted to be a barrister myself.

At playtime, a group of us formed a circle and started singing traditional Setswana songs. We used a box as an improvised drum and pulled down our dresses to make skirts, exposing our upper bodies. Then we took turns dancing inside the circle. Berka Solomon, who always seemed to be mysteriously positioned to run some errand or another for the Principal, came over and told us that we had to stop dancing.

'Why can't we dance?' I wanted to know.

'Because the Principal says you can't.'

'But why can't we?' I would not give up.

'Father James, the Roman Catholic Priest doesn't like it. They say it is the dance movements. Apparently the dance movements are un-Christian. Christian children don't dance like that.'

'But I don't understand? How do Christian children dance?' I knew about Father James' crazy idea about a white-bearded man in red who came down a hole in the roof on Christmas Eve bringing presents for all Christian children. But everybody laughed about that and dismissed it as the something that probably used to happen during the times of Adam or Jacob or the Twelve Disciples. The pictures of the animals the man supposedly rode showed some strange antelope with tree-like horns. And indeed no such man came through the hole in our rondavel roof. That just went to show that the story was no more than an old fable. Father James was generally given to telling all kinds of implausible tales.

The ban on dancing was something new to me, though. 'Well Monei, there is nothing to understand. You can't dance like that in school. It is not encouraged. Christian children do not dance like that. And you certainly should not pull down your dresses like that!

47

Pull up those dresses now and behave like civilised schoolgirls! This is not the cattle post!' The voice was that of Mr Thari, the Principal. 'Now come, all of you! You can all join the Girl Guides Club if you want to do something with your spare time. All of you come to my office so I can take your names down. The Girl Guides Club needs more members. Come on, hurry! I don't have all day!'

After that I had to stay on after school two days a week for the Girl Guides Club. I did not like the boring left-right, left-right marching. The songs were monotonous and had little relevance to my life. There was a song about California and another about American soldiers who went to the moon. And there was yet another about Dublin City and how there once lived a girl called Molly Malone, who pushed her wheelbarrow, through streets broad and narrow, crying cockles and muscles. Molly Malone, according to the song, was fair and pretty. I didn't know where Dublin was, what a city was and didn't really care whether Molly Malone was fair or unfair, but the Girl Guide teacher urged us to smile as we sang because, she said, it was a happy song. All the Girl Guide songs were in English, which we were struggling with at the time. To add to all that, my mother was not happy about having to convince my father to part with money for yet another uniform. And there were all these badges that had to be paid for. I really did not like the Girl Guides Club and wished I had never asked about Christian dancing. I really had to learn to contain myself, I decided, if I was going to survive school. I had to learn to pull back, not be at the head of the line. All I had done was ask a question and I ended up singing about Molly Malone; life was not fair.

This charging forward had been the reason why Sylvia hated me. I had discovered that someone had written something rude about Sylvia in the girl's toilets and I had immediately gone to report it to the Principal. It turned out that half the girls in the school had made the same discovery and said nothing. Only foolish me thought something had to be done about it. It also turned out that Sylvia had written the message herself, which perhaps half the school had suspected to be the case, anyway.

I really did try to drag my feet, slow my brain and keep down my hand, but I was not always successful. That was how I ended up in the Girl Guides Club marching to songs about far away places.

Father James, the Roman Catholic Priest, who discouraged traditional dancing as un-Christian, was an old man with skin fried by the sun to a reddish-brown colour. The back of his neck was wrinkled and was the same texture and colour as the little bag he carried everywhere. He was a sad-looking man who seemed to have little to smile about. But then how could he possibly ever be happy, with his favourite man Jesus hanging dead and bleeding. The Priest's eyes were watery and he was forever dabbing at them with a handkerchief. My grandmother said it was unnatural how the Catholic Church mourned the death of Jesus Christ forever. 'How can his soul rest in peace the way that Priest goes on and on about how he was killed on the cross? He talks about forgiveness one minute and then he is on about the Jews and their killing of Jesus Christ. He bears a grudge higher than Phaphane Hill over that killing, I tell you,' she would say.

Once a month Father James came to our school to lead us in prayers at morning assembly. He spoke in Setswana most of the time but his accent was so bad that no one understood much of what he said and often he jumbled up words. There was a time, for example, when he gave a long sermon about breasts. He told us about the importance of letting one's spirit grow and swell and ripen like breasts on fertile brown earth. We had tittered and whispered in response, even though we knew exactly what he had wanted to say. *Mabele* for sorghum and *mabele* for breasts were always causing confusions for foreign tongues and Father James was no exception. After that we called him Father Breasts until the Principal found out and banned the name. He knew better than to allow a nickname to flourish for he suspected, correctly, that he had one himself.

The few times Father James spoke in English, the Principal had to interpret but he largely made up the sermon. This was on account of the Principal's not-so-great English and Father James' Irish accent. I think the Principal didn't like Father James coming to our school but for some reason he was not able to stop it. It was never clear to us how Father James had the power to meddle in school matters.

Father James would dab at his teary eyes and blow his red bulbous nose, with its hairy innards, noisily. He also had hair sprouting from his ears and I had once observed a louse leisurely weaving its way amongst the hairs. But before I had an opportunity to show the louse to Mary, the louse had disappeared into the recesses of the ear and she refused to believe me. White people simply did not have lice, she maintained. She said it was a well-known fact so I did not mention the louse spotting to anyone else, lest I be called a liar. Father James complained of some illness called hay-fever, but there was no hay in the village or, at least, I had no idea what hay was. And whatever it was, it did not seem to give anyone, except Father James, a fever. I just figured he was embarrassed that he was always sniffling about the death of Jesus Christ. I figured it was perhaps on account of all those sad stories he told, about people he obviously cared about, who got killed or chased out of their land. There was a lot of misery in the Bible. People moving to new places, women with no children, women stealing each other husbands and brothers hating each other and stealing each other's luck. The characters in the Bible were a confusing bunch. Just as you started to like one of them, he or she did something really mean. Right from Eve, ungrateful Eve, who, after Adam lost a rib to her creation, turned around and led him astray. But it was when he recounted the death of Jesus Christ on the cross that Father James' voice quivered most. It seemed like Jesus had failed to answer a few simple questions and the Jews who wanted the answers took the matter too seriously and hung him and then nailed him to a cross. And he was a Jew too! Centuries later, Father James was still upset about this death and he was Irish. It was not clear how the Irish and the Jews were related. Father James never explained that connection.

There was also the confusion of what Jesus exactly said on the cross that seemed to sadden Father James. Did he call for the forgiveness of the Jews or did he doubt his God? In any event, on the third day he rose and went to Heaven, so the story ended well enough so Father James should have been happy. On the whole though, the story didn't sound believable. It had the same ring as the many stories we were told at home, about Dimo, a giant who bagged disrespectful children and roasted them for dinner. Still,

Father James sniffled as he raised his hands to Heaven entreating, 'Believe in the Lord Jesus Christ, and your sins shall be forgiven.' My grandmother said Jesus Christ was a good man with good ideas, although he could be rude on occasion. 'He had no cause to talk his parents like that when they asked where he had been. They were worried about him and they had cause to be! No child, no matter how famous, has a right to talk like that to his parents!'

And I did say prayers in the name of Jesus Christ occasionally. I had long ago decided to add him to my ancestors and God, figuring an additional protector could not do any harm. And he had protected my secret from Mrs Monyatsi, hadn't he?

I was actually a bit afraid of Father James. This was primarily on account of stories of a Catholic father in Kokoto, a neighbouring village who, it was rumoured, took little girls on trips to the country and prayed for them as he touched them all over, entreating them to accept the Lord with their entire beings. The prayers ended up with him shivering and breathless and almost fainting. It was not clear what was wrong with his praying methods, but there was certainly secrecy and shame involved. I decided that if ever Father James even looked remotely like he was about to change his praying methods, or if he suddenly acquired a taste for open fields, I would be out of that church before he could say 'Eloi, Eloi, lama sabachthani'. I was not about to let him shiver all over me, even if that would ensure me a place in Heaven.

My grandmother said Father James had learnt Setswana because he had come to persuade, while the other white people in the village had not bothered to learn the language because they had come to issue orders. She said this as a compliment to Father James, even though she swore he would never persuade her. 'He is a good man, that Father James, if a bit strange. Although if he took a wife his energies would be more balanced and he wouldn't be so sick all the time. Any fool can see that redness and sniffing is from clotted blood. Well, it's not for me to say what's good for a white man! And I'm not too sure that he should be allowed to teach young children. I think Christianity should be taught to adults only, because they already know what they believe in. Then we can argue and see who can convince the other. But I have to say that Jesus man was generally a good man.' My grandmother had endless views about the white man's religious teachings. She loved hymns and attended both the Roman Catholic Church and the Dutch Reformed Church fairly regularly. She declared herself perplexed that Mr Benjamin, the nice shop owner who lived near the railway station, did not attend church like the other white people. 'They say he is a Jew, and that explains why he does not go to church. Well, don't both churches go on and on about how Jesus was a Jew? If that man is anybody's ancestor, he is Mr Benjamin's ancestor. I don't know where the Irish fit in, but it seems to me that Father James is a bit confused about who he should be praying to.' 'But the Jews crucified Jesus,' I tried to explain. 'So? Why is an Irishman getting involved in Jewish matters then? Is he now going to adopt every ancestor killed by his own people? I know that Bible of theirs is big but I can tell you, Nei, child of my child, you are there, I am here, it cannot explain that! So the Jews killed their own son. That's bad, but who are these Irish to come here and bother us about it? But I have to say, Nei, that that Jesus fellow had some good ideas. He was a bit too nice though. You can't spend the rest of your life turning the other cheek. I have to say it depends who you are turning it to. Some people would just keep on slapping it! You could get pretty bloody cheeks if you don't think before following Jesus' teachings. He does say though that you must respect your mother and father. Good teaching that. Not that he always followed his own teachings. I'm not happy that he was so rude to his parents though! And didn't he overturn tables in some temple somewhere?' My grandmother said the worst white man ever was someone called Paul Kruger who, she said, had subjected the Bakgatla to humiliation at some time in the past. Sometimes she said that Paul Kruger was the single reason she would never truly believe in the white man's religion.

I preferred the Mother's Union women from the Dutch Reformed Church. They too came once a month to our school. They too read from the Bible and spoke about death, banishment, deceit and women who could not have children. They talked about women giving themselves to men to plant their seed. But they did not seem to be saddened by it all. In fact, they seemed positively jovial about the whole Jesus Christ matter. They smiled and swayed as they sang about his death on the cross. I thought that perhaps it was because of the rumours that some of the Mother's Union women were witches. Witches or not, they led the school in beautiful gay hymns. And it helped that they were Batswana and there was no need for any translations. In addition, their church was nicer. It was bigger and cooler and had stairs leading up to the main door. One of the pastors was a Motswana and I could hear everything he said, not that I could understand everything, though. The word of God was not always easy to understand and, unlike at school, I could not raise my hand to ask questions. There was that confusing story about Adam and Eve, especially since there was already another story about the first inhabitants of the earth that my grandmother told us. According to this version, the first people were Matsieng and his family, who had emerged from the belly of the earth and then proceeded to multiply, filling the world with human beings. And true enough, I had seen their footprints with my own two eyes. They had stepped on the newly formed earth, when rocks were still soft, and left their footprints forever. It seemed to me that the evidence of Maitsieng's existence, etched in stone by his huge left foot, was weightier than the evidence of Adam's existence, which was etched in Genesis and could only be seen by those with the special ability to read.

And Father James said bearing children was a punishment from God for Eve's wickedness, while my grandmother said child-bearing was a blessing from God and the ancestors. Father James' voice had quivered as he had quoted from the Book of Genesis on what God said to Eve after she had led poor Adam astray: 'I will greatly multiply your sorrow and your conception; In pain you shall bear forth children; Your desire shall be for your husband, and he shall rule over you.'

My grandmother had said to me on the same topic, 'Nei, to bring forth a child is the greatest desire of every woman. You have not known true joy, until this happens.' She did agree with Father James that men had the God-given power to rule over women but said Adam should have been embarrassed to blame a woman for his own errors.

It was never really clear if Father James or the Dutch Reformed Church ministers were including Africa as part of the world when they preached about all those people eating apples they were not supposed to eat and killing their brothers. Or when they talked about fathers who favoured some sons, causing untold misery to whole generations. The confusion was deepened by the fact that Egypt was part of Africa according to the World Atlas, a book that we consulted twice a week during the Geography lessons, but was a place in Heaven, according to the teachings of the Bible. So it was not clear how that which I learned during the Geography lesson was related to what the two churches taught.

But still I was fascinated by the Bible stories, even though the question 'why?' seemed never to be asked or contemplated by any of the messengers of the word of God. But then the question 'why' was generally considered rude, even at home, so we all just listened and tried to figure things out when we were amongst ourselves. The result was that the views of the more forceful amongst us became the 'correct' ones. As a result, the question of where Egypt was located was put to rest by Mary's assertion that there were two different Egypts, the Bible one and the Geography one.

Another thing about the Dutch Reformed Church that I liked was that, unlike in the Catholic Church, the congregation didn't have to respond to everything that the *moruti* said and we didn't have to keep on standing up and sitting down right through the service. And there was no confusing kneeling and cross-making when you entered the church. And there were no boys dressed in long dresses and ringing bells and acting like they were in some kind of slow play. You just had to sing beautiful hymns and say amen at the end of the prayers. Occasionally you had to say the Lord's Prayer out loud, but generally you could sleep off the session without the *moruti* noticing. I never slept though. I liked the stained glass windows, the hymns, the strange voice *Moruti* Moremi assumed when he was preaching, and the high ceilings. I also liked to watch the white side of the church and admire the hats of the white ladies. And the carving of Jesus mounted behind the altar in the Dutch Reformed Church was easier to look at than the marble one in the Catholic Church. The Dutch Reformed Church Jesus was made of wood so the blood oozing from Jesus' hands, feet and side was brown, not the bright red of the Catholic Jesus. And the Catholic Church's Mary's blazing heart, as she cried for her son killed for everyone's sins, was not easy to take. As a result, I only went to the Catholic Church when I was too lazy to walk the two kilometres to the Dutch Reformed Church. I had also decided that when the time came for me to be baptised, I would join the Dutch Reformed *Phuthagwana* and not the Catholic Catechism. I was a bit suspicious of the Roman Catholic incantations and mumbling in foreign tongues. There was also Father James' insistence on renaming members of his flock. He had, for example, rejected Calamity Sebego's name and instead promptly renamed him Pious Sebego. How one was expected to find their way into heaven with all this last minute naming was not clear. And Calamity had been a strong name. Everyone, including the teachers, had marvelled at how Calamity's mother, who had never been to school had come up with such a powerful name for her son. Then he was named Pious, a weak name that did not fit smoothly into a Setswana sentence. The result was Calamity was called Paeyaase, to smooth out the bumpy bits of the name and to make it flow. I had no plans of being renamed by a Priest who had little regard for how the name would sound outside his church. The Dutch Reformed *moruti* seemed more tolerant. I had observed a Charity, a Gladness and a Modise being baptised without first being renamed. No doubt the Catholic Priest would have insisted on a Rachel or Mary or Magdalene.

The Dutch Reformed Church held two services, the English one and the Setswana one. Batswana could attend both and we children generally did but the Europeans left after the English sermon, which was the earlier one.

But on the whole, I liked Sundays because it was forbidden to do any work on Sundays. One could miss church, but one could not do the wash or pound sorghum on Sundays. The only work allowed on Sundays was cooking and fetching water. And even then, we had to do just enough for the day's needs. Doing any other work on Sundays could result in representatives of the Mother's Union paying you a visit. That was embarrassing and a bit frightening on account of the rumour that some of the Mother's Union women were witches. On Sundays they dressed up in fierce looking black-and-white uniforms and carried Bibles and Hymn-books but, at night, they rode hyenas and baboons, naked. 'Young girl, you will roast in hell if you do not heed the Word of God,' would be the admonition, if you were found working on a Sunday. Looking up at the stiff black cape, the offender could sense the other undeclared threat, 'I will come for you tonight and my hyena will gobble you up.'

But if the Mother's Union women did not get you, a worse fate still could befall you. God might snatch you and slap you on the face of the moon, for all to witness your sins. On the nights that the moon was full, we could see a man pulling a thorn bush on the moon. God had placed him there for the whole village to see, for he had dared chop thorn bushes for his kraal on a Sunday. His family has been disgraced ever since. I had no plans to join that man and I knew my friends felt the same way. So on Sundays, we happily played games, visited relatives and did no work.

CHAPTER 6

I was walking from the Catholic Church with my friend Kabo.
Knowing that we had hardly any errands to do at home and a bit
hungry, Kabo suggested that we go hunting for *borekhu*, that is
resin or gum, from the *modubu* trees along the river. The best resin
was from the *moselele* trees but there were none on our way home.
In any case, *modubu* trees may not have produced quality resin,
but they did beat *moselesele* trees in terms of quantity. But then
there was the issue of the location of *modubu* trees. They were
found along the river and the river harboured many dangers. A
sethula, called Rra-Vaselina, because he smeared the butts of his
victims with Vaseline before raping them, was said to operate
along the river. And then there was the ghost of Shinana, a boy
who had fallen from a tree while picking and collecting resin from
the big *modubu* tree in the middle of the river. Then there was a
kgogela, a snake-human that could pull a child into the river by
holding on to the victim's shadow.

'Should we? We have been warned not to stick around the river
without an older person,' I responded, not without trepidation.

'Come on, there is no Rra-Vaselina. My brother Thabo says that
the rapist is in Francistown, far, far away from here. The adults just
say that to scare us.'

'You sure? I am not afraid of Shinana's ghost. Ghosts are afraid
of the sun. As for the *kgogela*, we can just watch our shadows. But
the *sethula* frightens me.' Looking back, I have to say that life was
full of frightening beings, or at least that was what we were always
told. The rising moon, called the red knife, teachers, the chief, the
police, and witches were just some of the many beings we were

threatened with. There was even Mma-Meno, an old woman who lived alone and kept kindling under a huge pot, ready to be lit, just in case your mother brought you over for a roasting. A threat to be taken to Mma-Meno was enough to bring on good behaviour. She had impossibly white, straight, and sharp teeth, obviously cleaned and sharpened by years of feasting on young children.

'There is no *sethula* in this village. Those are just radio news stories in other places.'

'Promise?' I was still not too sure sticking around the river was a great idea.

'Yes, I promise you.'

'Swear by something important.'

'I swear by the red book at the Dutch Reformed Church.'

'No, that is not enough. Swearing on the Bible is not enough. It has to be something closer to you.'

'May lightning strike me if I am lying.'

'Swear by the fontanel of your sister's baby. May it stop pulsating if you are lying to me.'

Kabo did not blink as he pronounced solemnly, 'I swear by the fontanel of Naniso. If I am lying, may it stop pulsating.' He even added, '*Marete a pitse mapepene!* May I be struck by lightning if I'm lying.' He quickly drew a cross in the sand, circled it and spat into the middle.

I was convinced that indeed the *sethula* scare was just that. Clearly my friend was telling an unmitigated truth. No one would swear by the fontanel of any baby, especially one so close to him, unless they were telling the honest truth. And his swearing on the exposed testicles of a horse – *Marete a pitse mapepene* – and daring lightning to strike him told me that he was indeed very certain of his facts. Assured that no serious danger lurked behind the bushes, we spent the rest of the morning climbing one tree after another happily picking and eating *borekhu*.

When we could not stand the thirst anymore, we drank from the river. We were both aware of the repeated warnings at school against drinking river water. We were not even supposed to swim in it. But, when one's throat was parched and the gum was sticking to one's teeth and there was water right there shimmering in the afternoon sun, it was really difficult to heed these warnings.

On our way home we met Mmaletshiri, the old and demented woman who was supposedly the last person to be thrown into the witches' cave. She was also reputed to be the only person to ever survive the punishment. So, of course, all the children, including Kabo and I, gave her a wide berth. Upon sighting the old woman, her long tangled hair swaying from her jerky gait, we exchanged quick knowing glances and ran into the bush and hid behind a boulder.

'I see two little naughty children! I see two little naughty children! Should I have them for my supper?' The old woman chanted and then laughed out loud. Hearing this, we sprang from our hiding place and ran all the way home. We arrived panting and sweating and still scared that she might have flown after us. After all, she was a witch!

That would be the last day I saw Kabo until years and years later, when we were not children any more. The following day Kabo did not come to school and, when I went over to his house to find out what the matter was, I learnt that Kabo had been sent to the cattle post to drink milk for fattening and strengthening. Although Kabo had been losing weight and had been diagnosed with *setshwafu,* a condition causing the collapse of the area over the sternum, he had not seemed particularly ill.

'Mma-Kabo, when will Kabo come back?' I asked, close to tears.

Kabo had been my best friend since we had fought at the end of our first term of our first year in school. He had lent me his rubber, but I had chewed it up, absent-mindedly. During that first term in school, it seemed impossible for me to keep anything out of my mouth. I chewed on the back of my pencil and the ends of my rulers. I chewed on papers and even occasionally sucked my thumb. I had not even realised that I had Kabo's rubber in my mouth, until he started screaming at me to spit it out. The commotion had landed both of us in trouble with the teacher, earning us two strokes each on our buttocks with a cane. At the end of the day, Kabo made an appointment with me for an end-of-term fight. Classmates were informed and for three full weeks I sized up my opponent, noting his stout body and wondering how I was going to fare. I tried to start a rumour that Kabo was fighting a girl because he was afraid of fighting a boy, but the cause of the fight was considered to be justification enough. I suspected that the fight was the only one scheduled for the end of the term and the audience was not about to have it cancelled on a mere principle.

When the day came, I fared very badly indeed, leaving the fight with torn clothes and scraped knees and elbows. At least I had had the good sense to take off my uniform and fought only in my underwear, otherwise I would have had plenty of explaining to do when I got home. A torn uniform is not something that I would have wanted to bring home. Except for blood running down his right cheek, where I had scratched him, Kabo hardly seemed like he had been in a fight. I had not been able to throw him to the ground. It was a good thing that, as a boy, the rules prohibited him from scratching, otherwise I would have fared even worse. After the fight though, we became very good friends. He even gave me the rubber that I had half chewed up.

'He may come back next term. He needs milk and meat to give him strength. He is too thin for a boy.' Kabo's mother responded.

'But what about school? Why didn't he tell me he was going away?' My voice was trembling. My best friend had not bothered to say goodbye. I also knew that mid-term cattle post visits often ended up with the boy not coming back to school.

'He didn't know he was leaving, Nei. Even I didn't know. His father sent word that he should be sent with Kereng's tractor and I only got word of that last night, when Kereng's men came to pick Kabo up. I, too, am missing him already.'

'But do you really think he will come back next term? Do you promise?' I was desperate.

'Nei, Kabo is a boy. You need a girl friend. A girl should have girl friends. Otherwise people will think Kabo is just a girl. But I hope he will come back. The decision is not mine, though. The decision rests with his father, my child.' Mma-Kabo smiled at me kindly and I thanked her politely and walked back home.

I had homework, so I turned my mind to school work in an effort to forget my loss. The homework was a composition and we had to choose one topic and write three pages on it. The four choices were: 'A Beautiful Summer Day', 'A Visit to the Dentist', 'A Long Journey' and 'My Worst Nightmare'. As we had prepared to leave the classroom, Mrs Moloi had advised against the dentist topic, because, as she explained, since none of us had ever seen an eye doctor, we were unlikely to have anything to say on that topic. Martha whispered that a dentist was a tooth doctor, not an eye doctor but, when Mrs Moloi reprimanded her for whispering in class, she promptly shut up. Apparently there were doctors in Johannesburg who treated only specific parts of the body, even possibly in Gaborone and Mafikeng. It seemed a waste of money to have a doctor treating only eyes or teeth.

I chose to write on 'My Worst Nightmare'. As it turned out, I was the only one who wrote on this topic as no one had any clue what a nightmare was. Mrs Moloi was so impressed by my composition that she not only read it to the rest of the class, she read it to the whole school at morning assembly. It earned me the honour of wearing a white ribbon for an entire week. A white ribbon was worn around the left wrist as a mark of brilliance and usually it was just for a day. A week's wear was indeed a great honour.

The story I wrote was about a beautiful mare that was born in the middle of the night to a shiny black horse called Dash. I have to admit that it was a very involved story. It was a night mare because it was a horse born on a rainy night. As I had no idea about delivering horses, I wrote my grandmother into the story, making her the midwife. I called the mare Dashling and wrote up a great life for it. By page three, I had my grandmother being taught how to ride by a young prince called Kabo. Kabo was the son of a chief from a village in a mountain range far away. He had chanced upon us as he was passing with his entourage of magnificently clad young men and women. I ignored the three-page instruction and went on to pages four and five, and by that time, my grandmother and I were riding Dash and Dashling, camping by the side of the road, on our way to Francistown. I concluded, 'Two years after that terrible night, Dashling had grown into the most beautiful mare in the world. Therefore my worst night mare is now a beautiful mare, day and night.' It was not until I was in high school that I realised that I had completely missed the point with that assignment. So had Mrs Moloi and the whole school. Or perhaps I had been humoured, although I very much doubt it. What that story did though was to help me survive my worst nightmare, the disappearance of my best friend, Kabo. Being given to weaving my realities into dreams, there were times when I could actually pretend Kabo was still around.

CHAPTER 7

Kabo did not come back. Not the following term, and not the term after that. Later, I learnt that Kabo's older brother had had to leave for the mines to earn money for the family. There were taxes to pay and a new plough to be purchased and the brother was eighteen years old and strongly built. He was an excellent candidate. Shortly thereafter, Kabo's father fell ill and Kabo had to take over the care of the family cattle. When we next saw each other we were both twenty-three years old; I was on vacation from architectural school in London and he was on vacation from the gold mines in South Africa. He had turned into a handsome, strong muscular man. He had not lost the twinkle in his eye and he still laughed with his eyes long before his teeth caught up. But when they did, in place of the perfect set of teeth he had as a child, there was a gaping hole. I remembered that I had heard of how he had lost his teeth in a mining accident. We had had little to say to each other and so, after pleasantries, we had gone our separate ways.

But for months after Kabo boarded a tractor-trailer in the middle of the night, I thought of him with his head full of the alphabet, and words and numbers that he could not use at the cattle post. He could tell the time by a watch but there could not possibly be even one watch out there. He could count and add and calculate square roots of numbers, but what use was all this in the bush? Kabo loved bridges, after the District Commissioner's son had given him a book full of drawings of all kinds and sizes of bridges. Allen, the DC's son, had been a thin, wiry red-faced boy who had spent three months in the village as punishment for something he had done in a boarding school in his native England. We had met at the Dutch Reformed Church one Sunday, when Allen had not sat with his parents and other white people on their designated seats. He had, instead, to the amazement of everybody in the church, walked in through the white entrance, walked past the white section and right through the church to the section occupied by the local people. The DC had walked over to his son, frowning in disapproval, and tugged at his son's jacket, but the young man had shrugged his father off. A few seconds later, Allen's little sister had followed her brother, only to be swept off the floor by her horrified mother, before she crossed over to the dark side. I had watched as, one minute the DC's wife was still and composed, and the next she was leaping into the air, one hand keeping her hat in place, the other snatching the two-year-old off the floor. It was one of the most exciting things to happen in church for many years. I thought it might have been as exciting as it must have been when Jesus overturned the tables in a church a long time ago.

Afterwards, Allen had told Kabo and I about Manchester, his village, and London, the big town he planned to run to as soon as he got back home. He had told us about his stacks and stacks of books, which his father expected him to read but which, he said with a smile, he had no intention of reading.

'Do you have any books on tall buildings?' Kabo had asked in halting English.

'I hate tall buildings,' Allen had responded with vehemence.

'Aren't all the buildings in London tall, though? You plan to run off to London, is what you said!' I had responded. I was excited to be speaking to a white person.

'Not so loud, Monei! Anyway, I have a book on bridges. I love bridges. Would you like to see my book on bridges?'

Neither of us could understand the interest in bridges. The only bridge we had ever seen was hardly impressive and we could not imagine a book full of pictures of bridges. But we were fascinated by the only white boy we had ever spoken to, so we made arrangements to meet the following Sunday, when Allen would bring his book on bridges.

Allen had come through as he had promised and Kabo had promptly chosen his future career. He was going to build bridges when he grew up! And even when our teacher tried to explain to him that, with only one river going through the village and seeing how we already had a bridge, he could not possibly make a living building bridges, he had insisted that that was what he was going to do. Then, two Sundays later, our new friend Allen mounted a goat, a thing anybody knew was totally foolhardy as goats did not tolerate being treated like donkeys and mules. The goat bucked, sending Allen flying into a thorn bush. That afternoon, he was put into a train headed north, the direction of Rhodesia, to catch a plane back to England. Whether he ever ran off to London, I never knew. Years later, when I was in school in London, I thought of Allen and wondered whatever became of him.

After Kabo left for the cattle posts, I would recall his bridge-building dreams and shed silent tears. He was unlikely to ever build bridges. Boys who dropped out of school ended up going to the mines in South Africa, just as girls who dropped out of school ended up being married off to them. I hoped that nothing drastic took place in my own family that could result in my being pulled out of school. My mother had my sister Keneilwe and my sister-in-law, the wife of my eldest brother, to help her at the lands. Mmadira had started to entertain dreams of working in Johannesburg, the City of Gold, where there was no difference between day and night, and where life was fast and beautiful. This concerned me because my mother would be losing a pair of hands. And I would miss her.

I wondered whether it was disobeying my parents and going *borekhu* hunting that had led to the midnight departure of my best friend. It was a well-known fact that not listening to one's parents could lead to all sorts of misfortunes. But perhaps it was the bad luck of coming across Mmaletshiri that had doomed them into separation. The saying that I heard almost every day was that, if a child does not heed the law of her parents, she will heed the law of the vultures. The law of the vultures brought death, simple.

I decided that it would be best to tell my mother about our *borekhu* hunting expedition to limit chances of further doom. Honesty, we were always told, was a way of setting things right. And I knew this from personal experience. The previous year, Noka and Sera, who had come to visit, had killed a monitor lizard for no other reason than that they were curious about the location of its liver within its long body. They had killed and skinned it, to Kabo's and my horror. They had examined its insides and made comparisons with the insides of goats and chickens, which they had killed and seen being killed on numerous occasions. Sera had seemed fascinated by various organs. She did not poke at them like Noka did but she actually touched and sniffed at them. She was a disgusting girl, in my view, and I was anxiously waiting for her to go back to her own home. Afterwards they had demanded silence about their daring act from Kabo and I.

Then, that evening, an angry sandstorm had engulfed our world, raging, roaring, tearing. I had huddled next to my father wanting but afraid to tell him what had happened during the day. At first I had kept quiet, hoping that the storm would blow itself out but, when I heard a frightening sound just outside the hut's doorway and realised that the old strong *morula* tree had snapped into two, I knew I could not keep quiet anymore. Just as quickly as it had started, the sandstorm gave way to streaks of lightning and a merciless rain that poured through the roof as if none existed. I shivered and looked at Noka and Sera hoping that one of them would say something. When it seemed clear that their tongues had been welded to the roofs of their mouths by fear, I resolved to speak. However, just as I opened my mouth to tell the truth, my father announced with sad confidence, 'Someone killed a monitor lizard today. Now our houses will be blown away and we will all drown. Or perhaps some daring witchdoctor has stolen a baby *kgwanyape*, the rain snake, and now we have to suffer from such an irresponsible act.'

'Father, it was Noka and Sera and I tried to tell them that…' My father silenced me with a look that I thought had the whole power of the storm in it. I even thought I saw lightning flashing from his angry eyes. He turned his gaze to his son, who told all they had done on the basis of that look alone. He was trembling as he stammered and stuttered.

The following morning, all three huts had lost most of their grass roofs, two goats were dead having been struck by lightning, and the yard was crawling with corn crickets. Then Noka received a walloping from a switch of his own choosing and an order for silence for rest of the day. He was not to cry or talk, but instead he was to use the day contemplating the lesson given by God and the ancestors. His choice of the switch, a long flexible one, and his ability to comply with the no-crying order after such a thrashing, were indications of how much he appreciated the seriousness of his offence. I too was petrified into silence.

Sera was not punished, but instead my father harnessed a donkey, mounted it, ordered Sera to mount behind him and rode away in silence. When I dared ask, my mother's response was that there were offences so serious that only the offender's father could punish. It was months before I saw Sera again and when I did it was at a wedding back in Mochudi and she was helping the men skin a cow. She seemed unreasonably interested in the cow's heart as she was examining it and fondling it. I was not about to sink my hands into all the blood and slime, so I went off to help make bread instead. In any event, I half-expected lightning to flash and strike me, if I so much as smiled at Sera.

The midnight disappearance of my friend, coming as it did soon after the *borekhu* expedition and the meeting with Maletshidiri, had the hallmarks of God and ancestor interventions. It could have been because he had eaten hailstones a week before, even though he was not a first born. But I somehow doubted that because he let the stones melt and only drank the water. The taboo related to the stones, not drinking the water, or at least that is how I reasoned at the time. So I decided to tell before things went from bad to worse.

'Mma-Monei, we went *borekhu* hunting yesterday,' I announced to my mother. I was eyeing her keenly, on the lookout for changes in facial expression. A narrowing of the eyes always meant anger while a raised left eyebrow could mean anything from skepticism to worry.

'Oh, that's nice. Just remember that you must never give *borekhu* to small children.' My mother did not pause from working on the basket she was weaving and there was no change in her facial expression. But a blank face could mean 'go ahead, fall into my trap', so I knew I was not home free yet. The advice about not giving *borekhu* to young children was nothing new, though. Almost every conversation with her included some advice about taking care of younger nieces and nephews.

'Mma-Monei, Kabo left for the cattle post last night,' I tried again. If there was a link between our escapade and Kabo's leaving, this was the time for Mma-Monei to say.

'I heard, my child. You will miss him. But then, this should give you a chance to find a girl friend. Kabo was getting too old to keep on playing with a girl anyway. He was sure to end up useless from hanging around with you. But I am sure you will miss him.' My mother had paused from her work and was regarding me speculatively.

'We went *borekhu* hunting at the river, Mma-Monei.' I thought perhaps I should clarify matters.

'Oh yes. That is where you find lots of *borekhu*. The river is low so that is not a problem. But you must always avoid river water. You will get bilharzia otherwise. Or at least that is what the nurses say. But for the life of me, I don't see how it is possible not to use river water. We use it to wash clothes, to mix earth to do our *lapa* walls and floors and boys have to get clay for their play cattle! How can we not use river water, I ask! It is so easy for them to say, "don't use river water!"'

'Mma-Monei, we met Mmaletshiri on our way home. Do you think she placed a curse on us? Do you think that is why Kabo had to go?'

My mother looked up and smiled and said, 'No, my child. Kabo had to go because he needs to be built into a man. His father wants to guide him on being a man. Mmaletshiri is just an unhappy woman who has lost her head. She is harmless.' I wondered how Mmaletshiri could possibly be considered by anyone as harmless. Perhaps my mother had not been listening to me. She did not seem the least bit concerned by our near fatal confrontation with the deadliest witch in the whole village.

'But *mma,* I am talking about Mmaletshiri! She was the last witch to be thrown into the witches' cave! She was the only witch to come back! Everybody knows that!' My mother was not taking my situation seriously.

'Let me let you in on a secret, my child. When people can't understand something, they create stories about it. Mmaletshiri is not a witch. Her real name is not even Mmaletshiri but Tebatso. She was a beautiful girl who married a brutal man. Two years into the marriage she went mad and has never been the same. Perhaps she retreated into madness to avoid remembering what happened to her. Or perhaps it was the only way she could get out of the marriage. Her husband had paid ten herd of cattle as *bogadi* but all died in a drought that impoverished everyone, so her father could not pay back the *bogadi* to her husband when Tebatso wanted out. So all those stories about her being a witch are not true. I tell you, you should have seen her as a young girl! She was the envy of all of us!'

I was surprised to learn all this and it did not make sense. 'But she is so old! She cannot be your age! What do you mean she was the envy of all of you?'

'She is not that much older than me, actually. She is only a few summers older than I am, as I recall. But she has had a rough life and she does not take care of herself. That is why she looks so haggard. And her name is on account of her long unkempt hair.'

'Mma-Monei, tell me about the witches' cave, please.'

'What do you want to know about the cave? A minute ago the cave scared you. Now you want to know more about it.'

'Were witches really thrown into the cave? Have you ever seen that happen? And how did the Chief really, really know someone was a witch? I mean really know for sure?'

CHAPTER 8

After Kabo's departure, for a while I found myself spending time with Mosweu.

Mosweu was, as his name suggests, white. He was pink really, with pinkish-white hair. He was pink because he was an albino. We became fast friends but we had certain rules. There were all sorts of beliefs about albinos. We believed they did not die like other people but rather disappeared mysteriously. Anybody who doubted this would be challenged to point out an albino's grave. If an albino hit you, even playfully, you would end up having an albino child. Therefore it was best to avoid albinos completely. One of our rules was that Mosweu would not hit me under any circumstances, lest I ended up with an albino child. And if he did, I could hit him back, thus reversing the curse. But being a boy, Mosweu had dreams of picking off a bird with his slingshot. Hanging around me could well jeopardise this dream, especially if he ever came into contact with my *makgabe,* a little skirt made of string and beads. So I promised him that I would never act in a way that could possibly get him in contact with my *makgabe*. It was Mosweu who had offered this, in exchange for my friendship. I had considered it fair enough and can only remember him hitting me only once. In response, I had unfastened my *makgabe* and hit him on the head with it. He was funny and made me laugh so, at least, the loss of Kabo was somehow eased.

Mosweu was a mean marble player and I was not far behind. We made a great team and there was a month when, between the two of us, we had more than fifty marbles. And about fifteen of them were actually real. Most of our marbles were made from melted plastic, rolled very fast into marble-sized balls. To maximise the chances of perfect balls, the plastic had to be as hot as possible and, to minimise chances of burning one's palms, the rolling motion had to be really fast. Therefore the results depended on the skills and the pain threshhold of the roller. We were both very good at marble-making and at playing so we could demand to play only with teams offering well-made marbles. The after-school marble playing was one of the fads of the year during which I made friends with Mosweu.

Another fad was swimming in the river, an activity forbidden not just by the school, the hospital, the Chief, but by parents as well. Besides the bilharzia concern, once in a while, a child drowned in the river. The river was an unreliable brown swell, which could be slow and languid one moment and a torrent of rushing water the next. The river was possessed by the unhappy spirits of the many people who had drowned in it. And, of course, in at least two places, there lurked the mysterious *kgogela*, always ready to snatch a child reckless enough to stand on the river bank, with her shadow falling into the river. The result was that every adult in the village had the right to thrash any child found swimming in the river. That did not stop my friends and I from frolicking in the muddy water though. It just meant that we had to keep a lookout and to run at the slightest indication of danger.

'Mosweu, are you joining us this afternoon? We are going swimming,' I whispered one day in class.

Mosweu's face fell, 'I can't go swimming. Surely you know I can't go swimming?'

'Why not? We just need one of us to keep a lookout and we can out-run any old person in this village! Come on, it's fun!' I urged.

Mosweu looked down as if embarrassed, 'It is not that, Monei. The other kids won't let me into the water because they are afraid of me. They don't want to be in the water with me!'

'Well, in that case, I'm not going swimming either! Let's go hunting for *mabere* then. We can roast them and eat them by ourselves.' The beetles were plentiful, on account of recent rains.

'Oh, Monei, I can't eat termites. I just can't eat any kind of insect. Or any small creature! I just can't.' I knew Mosweu was squeamish; he refused to touch frogs and was always saddened by any sick-looking animal. But I had not realised that he would not eat termites and stuff.

'Come on, it's okay. We can do something else. You know what we can do? We can go and help your mother rebundle the roofing grass. She has been working on that for days now. Or we can watch your little sister as your mother works.' I was keen to do something to make him happy. I just could not understand why the other kids were so mean to him. I had become so comfortable with him that I hardly noticed the difference between us.

'You will do that? You will hold my sister? Even though she is like me?'

'Of course, I will. You are my friend. I will just have to hit your sister back if she hits me. Not hard. Just a light tap to make sure I don't have a child, like, you know, that.'

'I give her a tap back as well, all the time. It's not easy being like me. I don't want to have children who look like me either.' Just then the bell rang and Mrs Moloi stepped in from the cool front step back to the hot classroom and dismissed us.

Within a year though, Mosweu was avoiding me, just as most of the boys were avoiding the girls. They had taken to playing in exclusively boy groups and would walk off in a huff if we so much as tried to talk to them. Some even started to swim in their *ditshega* or cupped their privates protectively whenever girls were around.

That was the year 1966, when my country got its name, Botswana, back. No longer would it have to use the long and strange sounding name, British Bechuanaland Protectorate. On a windy disagreeable day, we marched from our respective schools waving blue, black, and white paper flags celebrating independence and the right to reclaim our country's name. I have to say that my first thought, when I saw the new flags, was that they could have done better, in terms of colours and design. I thought, 'such boring colours and such simple lines!'

The Principal looked almost genteel in his dark blue suit, white shirt and blue necktie. And instead of the customary stick, he was carrying a flag. 'Isn't it nice that the Queen has sent a princess to celebrate with us?' he said as he turned to Mrs Tobane with pride in his beaming face.

'Isn't it nice that the Queen is too busy to be here herself? And who says this woman is a princess anyway? I wouldn't put it past the British to send us some woman off the street and pass her off as a princess. They don't take us too seriously!'

'Mrs Tobane, you are too cynical! Why didn't you join the men in the freedom square since you pretend to be so knowledgeable in political matters? Then you can shout about building schools and hospitals for all of us. After all, you talk just like a man! And I dare say you must keep these thoughts from these innocent children.'

Mrs Tobane would not be shut up. 'All I am saying is that I see no reason to jump around with joy, just because protection we never had is now being withdrawn, or that some distant relative of the Queen has chosen to take her aunt's flag home!'

'What do you mean, protection we never had. We needed the British protection!'

'Yeah, to protect us from their brothers the Boers! These tribes come here, fight it out in our land and, when they can't decide who has won, they decide that one of them will protect us from the other! Then, when it becomes clear that we are too poor to be of any importance, what do they do? They both decide, "give the natives back their name!" So now we march like the idiots we are, to celebrate all that!'

'It's thoughts like yours that have landed some people in prison in Rhodesia and South Africa.'

'And it's thoughts like yours that have consigned us to a life of beggars in our own land. Where is the independence we are celebrating, when my father is coughing blood with nothing else to show for his years of digging up treasures for the white man? And didn't my brother die in Johannesburg, when all he was asking for was the right to walk with dignity, like a man? Where was the British protection then? And if we were being protected from the Boers, how come we were ruled from Mafikeng, from South Africa?'

'How your brother died, I do not know. And I do not wish to say anything bad about the departed!' There was a suggestion that something bad was there to be said, nonetheless.

'Leave my brother out of this! Why are you defending the British? These people went to a party somewhere in Europe, we are told, and carved up Africa amongst themselves and you stand there and defend them? I can't believe you!'

'My history book tells me it was us who asked for British protection. And my history book tells that Africa was subdivided at a conference not a party!'

'Party! Conference! What is the difference? And who wrote the history books anyway? And were you there to say, "No, don't put the ruler there. Move it to the left. You are going through a whole village." Were you? No. They filed into a room and drew straight lines this way and that way with no regard for the people living where their rulers went. It's a miracle they did not slice up people!'

'Now you are being ridiculous! And I wish you would not speak all this politics in front of the children! They don't need your venom.'

'Well, aren't we celebrating independence? Isn't independence about speaking one's mind?'

'You know, I have a good mind to recommend your dismissal from this school. Your kind of talk is not good for young children.'

'You just try it. You will be sorry you ever even thought about it.'

'Principal, shouldn't we be moving on? The children are ready.'

'Of course, of course. Get Mrs Monyatsi to lead us in song please. These politicians can ruin your day, indeed!'

I would have liked for the Principal and Mrs Tobane to continue their arguments. One learned a lot from such exchanges, I had long ago decided. I would have wanted to know why my school, the local hospital and now the big hospital in Gaborone were all named after white women. Who were these women? But I wondered silently and dared not open my mouth. Instead I sang with the rest of the school, waving my little paper flag and marched to the centre of the village to celebrate my nation's independence. I didn't feel particularly independent, though.

Mary's uncle, Binto, reckoned that independence was a good thing. Black people, called tribesmen by the law on that point, could buy white man's alcohol and any man could speak his mind at the freedom square. It wasn't clear, he said, whether *khadi*, a berry-based traditional liquor, was legal. Although the District Commissioner would not come out clearly on that point, he was not sending out parties of policemen to raid homes suspected of brewing *khadi*. Apparently the government in Gaborone was too busy, figuring out which laws to keep and which ones not to keep, to be bothered by *khadi* brewing in the countryside.

'They are going to keep the witchcraft and the marijuana prohibition laws. Stupid politicians, I say! They will promise you everything under the sun, but they will not give us simple enough things!' he had said, grinning and shaking his head. His teeth were almost black from bean-leaf stew and cigarette and marijuana smoking, three things he loved.

'What witchcraft law?' Mary and I had chorused. Mary's uncle Binto was a fascinating person. I wasn't sure whether I liked him or not. There were times when he was a mine of information, ready to tell us all sorts of interesting things, then there were times when he would snore away, in the middle of the day, and bark at you if you so much as said 'hello' to him. He had been in a charming mood. He had even taken a bath within the last two days, judging by his reasonably bearable smell.

'The Queen had a law against calling someone a witch. You could go to jail for that. Not that anyone bothered to observe that law. And the District Commissioners were smart enough to ignore that particular law. Now these new politicians, the ones who will build rivers and schools all over the place, are keeping the law. Isn't that stupid. If someone is a witch, what are we supposed to call them? There isn't even a law punishing witches. Did you know that? You can bewitch anyone in any manner that you want! Send them lightning with the sun shining right above the District Commissioner's fontanel, and no one can touch you! No wonder the Americans are taking over the world. These British are really soft. Anyone who could be cowed by such a rag-tag army as the Boers better give power to a stronger tribe, is what I say. Let the Americans take over the world, is what I say!'

'Tell us about how the Boers beat the British, will you?'

'Who cares about that? I don't concern myself about the history of totem-less tribes. Please get me some fire, little Mary, Mother of Jesus. I need to light my cigarette before those stupid politicians

75

send their policemen after me. I have to say that is the stupidest of the laws to keep. Who was ever hurt by a little marijuana? Alcohol, perhaps, but never a little marijuana!'

'Why can't women speak at the freedom square?' I asked. I was already thinking that perhaps my grandmother could go and talk about the beating of children in schools.

'Did I say that women couldn't speak at the freedom square? I think they can. I'm not sure they can. I have to say it sounds strange though that women can speak at the freedom square. This independence is confusing a lot of things. But I guess the Queen does speak in freedom squares in England and she is a woman. Isn't she? Mary Magdalene, do you reckon I will get my little fire before I die?' He was always tagging some other Biblical name or idea to Mary's name and Mary loved it. But Father James had paid him a visit about the matter, calling it blasphemy and calling Mary's name in vain. Uncle Binto didn't care about Father James' likes and dislikes. He didn't believe in hell, but then neither did my grandmother.

'Nei, child of my child,' my grandmother had whispered one day, as I cleaned her chamber pot, 'that hell stuff is perhaps the stupidest part of the white man's religion. You think God could put us in this place, hard as it is and then send us to hell afterwards? There are only two places, this place and heaven. Perhaps white people go to hell but, I bet you, you will not find a Motswana there. Living here is hard enough, don't tell me there is a hell to face afterwards. Although I would feel happier knowing that Paul Kruger was in hell.' I was studying for my baptism at the time and it was hard to try to separate my grandmother's truths from the Dutch Reform truths.

'I don't think making white man's alcohol legal is good. Look at how it gets you rumbling and singing at night!' Mary had ventured. I hadn't known it was illegal and actually doubted the accuracy of Uncle Binto's information. If it was, no one was enforcing the law because, on Saturday mornings, Mr Khunuo and his friends could be seen in the only alcohol shop in the village, drinking away and playing *morabaraba* or cards, rather openly.

'Oh, Mary, wife of Joseph, don't say that to your uncle. Have respect for your uncle. A man can't sing? Is that what independence means? A man can't sing?' Then he started singing a song about a beautiful girl with dimples in her cheeks and how he had sent her messages of love through countless messengers but could not win her heart.

We had decided it was time to leave him to his singing and smoking. I didn't think there was a real chance of getting my grandmother to talk about our hard school life at the freedom square. It sounded like the freedom square was where promises were made, not where complaints were registered. And Uncle Binto was probably right, except for the odd woman, the freedom square was generally a place for men.

There were times when I thought life would be much easier if I drank bull's urine, learned how to whistle and took goat herding more seriously. Then I would think of the alphabet and numbers in my head and how they would all go waste. I had taken to reading and I was reading anything and everything I could lay my hands on. I would drag pieces of papers from under bush fences and read torn private letters, thrown away schoolwork, mail order catalogues and anything else I could lay my hands on. When the bush fences proved inadequate to satisfy my appetite for reading materials, I discovered the newly opened library. Then I was in heaven. I was almost always the only one in that two-bookshelf-haven. I had never seen so many books in one place and, by the time I finished primary school, I had read or looked through every one of them.

CHAPTER 9

One day two nurses came to our school and rumours about their mission started to fly. The first period of the day was delayed as teachers went to the Principal's office to meet with the nurses. The two nurses had walked into the school compound in their stiff white uniforms, and their strange white caps sitting impossibly on their heads, with hundreds of eyes watching them.

'They have come to give injections to all those with lice,' declared Mary. Mary knew a lot of things and made up what she did not know. She knew, for example, where babies came from, having learned about this most secret occurrence, from her uncle Binto. When it was pointed out to her that Binto was hardly a reliable source, seeing as he was almost always under the influence of marijuana, *khadi* or both, she amended her story. She had actually personally observed a *kgogela,* half-human and half-fish, deliver a baby to her mother, one night when she could not sleep. When she was challenged once more, and it was pointed out that a *kgogela* never left the river as it would surely die, she decided that, actually, the baby was brought by a bearded snake. Mary had invited anybody who doubted her story to her house to behold the evidence, her youngest sister, one week old and clearly a recent arrival. A few of us went over primarily because a new baby always filled us with wonder and we would never pass an occasion to see and hold a new-born baby. But even after viewing Mary's baby sister, I remained skeptical that there existed a bearded snake that delivered babies in the dead of the night. The baby had been real enough but Mary's uncle Binto had rolled his eyes, humming to himself as he lay in his double bed, parked under a tree because it was too big to fit through the door of his rondavel. It was even doubtful whether breaking the walls around the door would have been sufficient as the rondavel was as tiny as the bed was large. It was often said that one of Binto's piglets had long left the kraal – a polite statement about his apparent lack of sanity – and the euphemism was generally extended to any member of his family whenever they expressed a view not supported by common sense. By implication, Mary's contributions had to be taken with a pinch of salt. Insanity tended to run in families, we had been told often enough.

'Binto's niece is hardly a reliable source! Everyone knows that Binto is crazy and doesn't craziness run in families?' someone piped from the back of the class.

'No, they have come to give injections to all those with bilharzia,' argued another voice.

'You don't get an injection if you have bilharzia. You get forced to take the most awful pills. In fact…' The voice trailed off in response to a loud scrape as Shadrack pushed his desk forward aggressively.

Shadrack stood up and glared at the last speaker and growled, 'None of you know why the nurses are here, so why don't you just shut up.'

'You can't just tell us to shut up, you bully!' countered Kadimo, who was known to go into fits and to foam at the mouth at the slightest provocation.

'Shut up, or I will break your anus!' Shadrack barked and advanced towards Kadimo to drive the message home. Kadimo made a face, but he did shut up. He had flung himself against Shadrack once, only to end up with a bloody nose. Shadrack had both lice and bilharzia. Also, Shadrack had a filthy mouth, was big, mean and ugly and when he said shut up, you shut up. Shadrack was also stupid and he could not recite the multiplication table.

The multiplication table, for some reason, had to be recited with everyone standing up in four crescent-shaped rows. Shadrack stood in the back, reciting, 'Three times three, huh-huh, three times four huh-huh, three times five huh-huh.' His 'huh-huhs' were lost in the midst of all the other voices but no one was fooled. Basically, Shadrack came to school not to learn but to kick at the buttocks of classmates during the mathematics period, on the instructions of Mr Moile. He was at least three years older than our oldest classmate and toughened up, both physically and mentally, by years at the cattle post. He was a bully. As if that was not enough, Shadrack's arms and legs were covered with festering sores and it was believed that they were highly contagious. He was given to scratching them, causing them to bleed, without seeming to feel the pain.

Mr Moile, an ugly, big, sweaty man with a belly that was always fighting to escape from the confines of his under-sized shirts, started every mathematics class by giving pupils problems to solve. He had discovered Shadrack's special talents when once, trying to help him understand subtraction, he had posed this question to him: 'Shadrack, let's try this. If you had twenty oranges, and Thomas took five from you, how many would you have?' Shadrack had responded with vehemence. 'He would never dare! I would break his anus!' That answer gave Mr Moile an idea and, after that, the problems had to be worked out on the board by five students at a time. Shadrack's job was to kick anyone who got a problem wrong. Since Shadrack was too dense to know a right answer from a wrong one, Mr Moile had to shout, 'Kick Mary, make those buttocks jiggle,' or 'Kick Moses, make his thing wiggle' as the case might be. A lot of kicking took place in Mr Moile's class because working out a problem under the circum-stances was rather intimidating, even for the smarter members of the class. I had been kicked on numerous occasions by Shadrack, so I knew that making Shadrack mad was not a good idea at all. He would make your buttocks jiggle or your thing wiggle and he might even infect you with his oozing sores. Shadrack loved mathematics lessons. We all shut up and waited for Miss Bodiba, our class teacher.

I watched as Miss Bodiba left the Principal's office and noted that she was not carrying the radio even though the next lesson was supposed to be the English Radio Lesson. I was disappointed as I had been hoping to hear the next segment of 'The Family Wilsons'. During the last English Radio Lesson, Mrs Wilsons was baking an apple pie. I had a very vague idea what that was, but I definitely wanted to hear more about this family. They lived on a street and went to parks to walk the family dog and went to the ocean to swim. I was intrigued by the idea that a dog could be walked, which seemed to involve letting it run around while restrained by a short rope tied around its neck. And even Mr and Mrs Wilsons swam. Swimming was a dangerous activity in my life and adults definitely did not swim. And, of course, I had never seen an ocean. I could only imagine the lives of the Family Wilsons and I was fascinated.

'All the girls up, please. And form a line and proceed quietly to the *mosetlha* tree.' Under the *mosetlha* was where all big meetings took place. Years later, when I was at secondary school, I would think of that *mosetlha* tree as the equivalent of the school hall, albeit without walls.

Under the tree, the nurse talked to us about monthly bleedings, which she said happened only to older girls and women. She told us to expect the bleeding to continue for about five to seven days. During this period we were to use rags or newspapers to catch the blood. I was shocked by the information. I imagined myself bleeding to death. It occurred to me that, perhaps, Shadrack's bleeding sores might well exacerbate the monthly bleedings, if his foot ever came into direct contact with one's naked bottom. I very briefly considered dropping out of school to avoid the onset of monthly bleedings, but the prospects outside school did not seem too attractive, so I dropped the idea as quickly as it had popped into my mind.

'Frieda, what do you think of all that?' I asked Frieda afterwards. Frieda was older than me and knew quite a bit about all sorts of things. She was not loud like Mary, so you had to approach her privately to get her advice. Since encountering Binto with his lolling eyes, I was always checking Mary's answers against Frieda's, anyway.

'That was all nonsense. Nothing like that happens.' Frieda was very certain. She was not even slowing down. She was acting like the threat of bleeding for up to seven days was nothing at all.

I hurried after her and asked, 'But why would the nurses tell us that, if it's not true? The teachers seemed to agree.' I was puzzled and scared. Nurses in uniform didn't visit schools often and when they did, it had to be something very important. The last time they had come was to give TB injections.

'You know that now that we have independence the Queen is trying to confuse everyone.' Frieda was walking fast. It was after school and, no doubt, she had errands to run at home. She was a very responsible girl, Frieda. She was always helping her mother without being asked and when we would play and goof off after school she would hurry home. But still, faced with this impending bleeding, I didn't think any errand was important enough not to wait.

'But I still don't understand why...'

'Monei, just use your head. If every woman were to bleed every month for five to seven days, as those nurses say happens, wouldn't there be blood everywhere? The nurses said that different women bleed at different times. This would mean that, if you got ten women together, at least one of them would have to be bleeding at any one time. That is a lot of bleeding. No one can hide blood. If your mother and your two sisters were to bleed every month, you would know about it. I say this is just as stupid as Mr Moshana, the science teacher, saying the earth is round.'

'You mean you don't believe him? You don't think the earth is round?' I was confused.

'Come on Monei. Look around you. The earth is flat and any idiot can see that. And the sun goes around the earth. You don't have to go to school to learn that!' Frieda was looking at me like I was some kind of idiot. Indeed I felt like one.

'Then why are they telling us different in school?'

'Who knows? The important thing is to remember to write that the earth is round when asked. There is a lot of stuff you learn at school that is either not true or is just not important. They have just been told to teach us the stuff because it is in books from England. Maybe the English earth is round. Maybe women in England bleed every month. I don't know. How can I know English matters? But what I know is what I can see here, no matter what the books say.'

'I still can't see why...'

'Monei look, haven't we been told countless times that there are four seasons in a year?'

'Yes, we have winter, spring, summer and autumn.'

'But how many seasons do we really have? Not what the books say, but what you can see around you?'

'Two, winter and summer. Unless you want to reckon seasons according to the ploughing cycle, in which case we have three. That is, the ploughing season, the feasting season and the harvesting season.'

Frieda smiled triumphantly at me, 'There you are! But you can't say that on a Geography test. You have to remember to say there are four seasons. There are school facts and real-life facts. For example, an English cat says 'meow', but a Setswana cat says 'nngao'. In an English test, you can't write the real truth. You must remember the book truth. This is what I am trying to explain to you! So forget about that monthly bleeding stuff.'

'But I still don't understand why…' I trailed off in confusion.

Frieda stopped and faced me, pursing her lips to demonstrate her exasperation. 'Look Monei, what's written in books is school truth. What is spoken and is obvious is the real truth. That is why, although my real name is Lesego, at school I'm called Frieda. That is the name in the book. That is why Mr Rabana can't live with both his wives at the teachers' quarters. Only one wife is allowed to live with him.'

'Why?'

'Well you can only have one Mrs Rabana. That is what the books say – Mr and Mrs Wilson. Mr and Mrs Malden. You can't have Mr and Mrs and Mrs Wilson. You just can't. But maybe, now that we have independence, he can bring his other wife to live with him. I don't know about that. But I don't think so, really. I don't think a president can change English things like that. Anyway, I have to go. I have errands to run at home.'

With this explanation, I put the nurse's teachings out of my mind. I thought of asking my grandmother but I couldn't imagine her knowing nurse matters. In any event, I couldn't really imagine bleeding continuously for five days. It was so scary that I decided that it could not possibly be true.

Two weeks later, Mary stood up from the pit latrine and I was shocked to see a drop of bright red blood shimmering on the toilet seat.

'Oh my God, you have a bad case of bilharzia, you must go to the hospital.' I had had bilharzia but it had not been that bad at all. Mary was going to die if she did not get help quick.

'Hasn't your aunt spoken to you about this? Or your grand-mother? She seems to tell you lots of things.' Mary responded without alarm.

I frowned without comprehension. I didn't know how aunts and grandmothers came into bilharzia conversations. When I didn't answer, Mary assured me that she would go to the hospital at the end of the week. It sounded to me like she was putting me off. I was agitated; I had never seen such a bad case of bilharzia.

'I think you should go today. Now! Ask for permission to leave now!' I was upset. Even my brother, Noka, who had a bad case of bilharzia had not had it this bad.

'I will go, Monei. After school. I will be fine until then.'

Mary seemed rather calm about the whole matter. She seemed even calmer than when, a month previously, she had put her hand into her school uniform pocket only to remove it with a scream. She had promptly taken off her dress and our investigations had revealed a scorpion in the pocket. She had taken off her dress in total disregard of the fact that she was not wearing any underwear and there were dozens of schoolmates around. Even after she had put her dress back on, she had been uneasy, as if expecting a whole nest of scorpions to attack her. The truth was that scorpion stings were unpleasant but, unless it was the big black hairy one, you didn't expect much to happen to you. I had been stung twice in my lifetime but I would have walked gently until I got home before taking off the dress, especially if I had had to wash my only pair of panties that morning, as she obviously had done. But, had I stood up from the toilet seat, leaving a shilling-sized drop of blood, I would have left the toilet howling for my mother, certain I was about to die. Mary seemed unnaturally calm about the blood matter.

Before the end of the year, Frieda started to thicken around the waist and then, finally, she could not squeeze into her school uniform anymore. She dropped out of school and soon thereafter she had a baby. There were whispers around the school and our ward that Frieda had done bad things with boys. Frieda was fourteen when she did the bad things. I was eleven at that time and in Standard Three. As I later found out, Frieda's condition could be traced back to a night of playing hide-and-seek with her age mates in the ward open space. Frieda was not in my ward, so I was not present during the hide-and-seek game. But I was told that Frieda had run into a neighbour's yard to hide but more than just hiding had taken place. So it was not a boy, but rather a man who had been responsible for Frieda's condition. The man was made to pay six heads of cattle for causing the collapse of the breasts and diminishing the marriage prospects of one so young and innocent. Frieda's older sister was pulled out of school as well and married off before her eighteenth birthday. The family had hard evidence that educating girls was a waste of time. Frieda's mother expressed the view, rather bitterly, that school-going girls seemed to become pregnant rather easily. Perhaps it was the *maluti,* the American food the children ate at school, my Unlce Fifi had pondered. Something in the yellow maize was making young girls particularly fertile, he had opined. Luckily for me, my parents were not persuaded by the arguments and thought perhaps it was on account of Fifi's wife's third confinement, and the need for a young girl to run errands for the new mother, that Fifi was arguing for my removal from school.

'It seems to me that a man who should have known better, and not yellow maize, is responsible for that poor child's condition,' my mother had countered tersely. But then she had added with raised eye-brows, 'I dare say that maize could possibly be yellow was a surprise to me. Not that I think it has anything to do with the girl's troubles!'

'And if she were my daughter, his wife would be wearing a black dress and his children would be orphans!' my father added.

'I still say there is something suspicious about this American yellow maize. Who ever heard of yellow maize?' my uncle Fifi retorted.

My father had shaken his head and replied, 'Who ever heard of a man grabbing a child from play to satisfy his nasty lust? If children cannot play with their age mates in the moonlight where can they play? Well, thanks for your concern, man of my tribe, but Monei is staying in school. Mark my words, the educated will inherit this land.'

Without Frieda to advise me, I started to believe that the earth was round and that there were four seasons in Botswana, just like in England.

When my grandmother woke me up one early morning and told me about the monthly bleedings, I realised there were some school truths that were also home truths. After the talk, she told me to take a broom and to brush over my chest as I leaned over the large clay pot at the back of the rondavel where we slept. This was to sweep away the small buds of breasts I had started to sprout. This would delay their growth and postpone the onset of the bleedings for months, perhaps even years. There was no need to hurry into adulthood, she told me.

I took a very keen interest in science and mathematics. I liked the experiments, although I could not see how they would be useful in real life. The most complicated piece of machinery I had ever used was a radio and the most sophisticated building I had ever seen was the Dutch Reformed Church, with its fifteen windows and huge doors. So a lot of the information about electric power, sound and light was completely foreign.

CHAPTER 10

Just as rumours about Frieda and the bad things that she had done died down, my own sister Mmadira came home from Johannesburg, South Africa, with a distended belly and a long sad face. At first she had refused to say anything about her condition, crying endlessly whenever our mother sat her down for private discussions. My grandmother muttered that no girl was ever safe in fast Johannesburg, but my mother answered that it did not seem that any girl was safe anywhere. My father was silent and pensive and my sister Keneilwe was extremely responsive to Mmadira's needs. She cooked her special foods and would not let her do such heavy work as stamping sorghum. She whispered to her, telling her that everything would be fine. She promised to help her with her troubles and assured her that only good would come from her condition. It seemed to me that a lot of cagey words were used when I was around.

Mmadira had been eighteen when she first did a *motshela-kgabo* or monkey crossing into South Africa. Monkey crossings, that is, jumping over the fence like a monkey, were common because that was the only way Bakgatla could go back to their land, across a political border they had never really accepted, if they did not have a passport. Many were not keen on the long process of obtaining a passport or limitations on their stay in South Africa, so they simply did not bother to obtain documents. The crossings were called monkey crossings also because the Bakgatla's totem is the monkey. Monkey crossings were dangerous because, if the Boers caught the offender, she or he could be beaten and killed or beaten and sold to a farmer to work for up to a year with no pay, little food and no access to life beyond the farm. But Mmadira was good at monkey crossings, so she was never caught. But after a few such crossings, she decided the risks were too much so she did get a passport. She bought it for a chicken and a bucket of beans from a friend who got married and did not need it any more. In the passport, her name was Johanna Modise but, since having more than one first name was common enough, which confused the authorities, and a surname was an invention of the authorities, which the Batswana still found confusing, no one in authority was ever the wiser. The attitude of the authorities was that the natives could never decide on one name, anyway, so what if the woman called Johanna was answering to some other name when speaking to her companions. What if it took more than one calling of her name to get her to the head of the queue? There was a resemblance between the two women but it did help that, whenever she crossed the border, Mmadira always wore the same clothes her friend had worn when her passport photograph was taken.

Just one day before Christmas, three days shy of her 20th birthday – her birthday was easy to remember because it was two days before Christmas day – Mmadira arrived from Johannesburg. She had with her two suitcases, three loaves of bread, a box of dried peanut-buttered slices of bread, two cans of groovy soft drink and a few baby clothes. The suitcases and the box also harboured bedbugs, but that was common enough. Johannesburg was a place where people came back from with a bit of money, new clothes, a bit of food and bedbugs.

A few months later, Mmadira complained of pains in her tummy. I suggested that she take something to relieve the constipation, but no one was impressed by my suggestion. Instead, Noka and I were dispatched to Mma-Sera's house with orders not to return until told. Worried about my sister, I came up with all sorts of reasons to come back home. First, I had forgotten my schoolbooks, then it was my shoes, then something else. My cousin Sera said Mmadira was going to have a baby. That didn't seem likely since she was not married yet, and I had not seen any family meetings with any family about the matter, and I certainly had not heard of any rumours of a hide-and-seek game that had resulted in more than hide-and-seek happening. The onset of a marriage and the arrival of a baby were always preceded by endless early morning meetings, at which firm words were exchanged and cows were discussed. None of this had happened. Anyway, Sera was kind of strange with her interest in insides of bodies. She had failed to persuade me to lie back so she could feel and locate my organs. So, I wasn't surprised when she tried to confuse me with her suggestion that my sister was about to have a baby.

For two days Mmadira grunted and writhed with pain and, at the end of the ordeal, to the amazement of the mid-wife and my grandmother who had seen many strange things in her long life, produced a white baby. At first, the baby was thought to be an albino but, on further examination, it was determined that the baby was white, as in having been fathered by a white man. My grandmother named her Sediko, meaning full circle, the significance of which was lost on me. My mother named the baby Mmaleburu, meaning 'Miss Boer' or 'Mother of a Boer'. Mmadira named her daughter Kgomotso, 'she who comforts me'; an aunt named her Diphetogo, 'developments'; an uncle named her Montlenyane, 'the little beautiful one'; and I named my niece Naledi, meaning 'star'. A toddler cousin offered her own name, Lebebe and, when asked what she would herself be called, she answered, to everyone's amusement, that they would share the name. '*Mme* says we must always share,' she explained proudly. But the baby was promptly nicknamed Dutchgirl and that was the name that was used more often than all others put together.

Mmadira herself had lost most of her light complexion having long run out of her one tube of the skin-lightening cream, Ambi Extra for Men, she had brought from Johannesburg. She had to use the male version on account of her stubborn dark colouring. Ambi Extra for Men promised its users a light complexion and Mmadira, like many black men and women working in South Africa, paid for this dream of near-whiteness. But now, blackness had reasserted itself so that, when she placed her hand on her cheek in sadness at what had befallen her, there was uniformity of colour between the back of her hand and her face. It didn't seem like it had during her light-face/dark-hand days, that some stranger was holding her cheek. But when she held her baby to her breast, it did seem like she was feeding a stranger's baby.

The white baby created all sorts of reactions. White babies did pop up on occasion, after women had come back from Johannesburg, but still it was something that happened to other families and was whispered about. The Boers had publicly whipped a chief of the Bakgatla. It was a generation or two ago, but time did not seem to dim that memory. So consorting with Boers was not a thing that pleased the average Mokgatla. Within hours of the baby's birth, the ward and beyond was abuzz with news of the occurrence. Relatives and friends we had not seen for months suddenly came to visit.

My father fell silent and sad. He went off to the cattle post for three full months, during which time he spoke to no one. My mother hovered around the baby with wonder and worry. She had never taken care of a white baby and she had no idea whether the traditional herbs for babies would help or harm her. The practice was to shave a newborn baby's head, but most white people were known to keep long hair. Would shaving a white baby harm it? Then the baby fell ill after an aunt, who could only have been menstruating, had been allowed come in to see the mother and baby while they were still in confinement. My brother Noka was dispatched to go and dig up the necessary roots to counter the effects of the aunt's visit and when, within two days, the baby was well again, it was clear that traditional herbs did work on white babies. This was a major relief to my mother. In fact, when the baby was four months old and her mother had gone off to collect firewood, a cousin with a nursing baby thought nothing of offering her own breast to calm the screaming Dutchgirl. And she latched on, like an ordinary baby.

My age mates, cousins and friends loved the strange baby. It was like having a living doll. The few dolls in the few shops were white and now we had one of those to play with. The only drawback was that even white babies leaked from all ends and needed care in that respect. So the baby also meant an extra chore for me. Still, I was the envy of my friends, for none had a niece like mine. I was the baby's youngest aunt, the only *mmane,* younger mother, she had. My pride knew no bounds. That was before Keletso was born and stole my special place in life and before my grandmother died, leaving a gaping hole in my heart.

After the birth of Dutchgirl, Mmadira cried and cried for days. Silent tears she tried to hide as she lay in seclusion with her new baby. She stared at the watch that she said her boss had thrust, almost angrily, into her hands when she told him about the pregnancy, the result of urgent mid-morning returns from work when the lady of the house had gone for church meetings. When Mmadira had threatened to tell the boss's wife, the boss had threatened to kill himself, a threat Mmadira had taken seriously enough to pack her bags and leave without one word to the woman with whom she had shared a bed and a man, albeit in turns. She had decided that she would have enough struggle to raise the new life without contributing to ending an old one. There had been relief in the eyes of Mr Malan, she said, as he waved good-bye from the steps of his lavish family home. He didn't have to kill himself after all.

'Mmadira my child, don't cry. You will give the baby bad luck,' my mother rebuked gently.

'What am I going to do with a white baby, *mma*? I don't know how to take care of a white baby.' There was dismay in Mmadira's voice.

'Come on, my child. Wipe away those tears. A baby is a baby, white or black. Look, she is thriving. You should be happy. A sad heart will make your milk bad for the baby. Even white babies can sense a sad mother. A mother should be happy.'

'But *mma,* you know that white children are all ill-mannered and mischievous. They fight people and are bullish. The De Villiers boys are notorious in the whole village. Their sisters are no different. They smoke and curse and laugh like jackals. What am I going to do with a child like that?'

My mother had shaken her head. 'My child, a baby is what you, as its mother, make it to be! If you let it run around like a scoundrel and give it no direction then, of course, it will end up ill-mannered and mischievous. You think those De Villiers children are wild because they are coloured? No, my child, they are wild because they have been allowed to run wild. No direction from those foul-mouthed parents of theirs.'

Mmadira managed a small smile and said, 'You really think so? You think that Kgomotso can grow into a nice well-behaved girl? Even though she is coloured?'

'Of course, she will. Come, it's time for your bath. The sun goes down early now that it is winter. If you don't get moving, it's going to be cold out soon. And stop being so sad. Sad milk is not good for a child. She will know you are not happy with her and she will not get strong and healthy. A baby must feel a happy mother's heart when feeding.'

'Okay *mma,* let me feed Kgomotso one more time before I take my bath.'

'She is asleep. Let her sleep. She will be fine. Come, let's go my child. The water will get cold if we don't move now.'

Mmadira took a blanket and covered herself from head to toe and followed our mother out. As a woman in confinement, she could only leave the house to go and relieve herself and to take her daily baths. And even then, she had to use the chamber pot for urinating. And when she did venture out of the rondavel, which she had to try to make sure was after sunset, she had to be covered to avoid being seen or coming into contact with anyone who might harm the baby. The baths could be planned for just after sunset, but sometimes nature called at awkward times, in which case she had to go out during daytime. Then she was a slow moving, feet shuffling, head-to-toe-covered figure. As for me, I remained in the rondavel, watching the mysterious baby and marvelling at her long brown fine hair.

The bathing place was behind the five rondavels, at the back of the *lapa.* Mmadira enjoyed the daily baths because they were more than just baths. They were really massages and she would receive them for three months, that is, during the entire period of her confinement. Sometimes I was jealous of my sister, all this attention from our mother. At such times, I thought perhaps I should go and ask Frieda if she could arrange for me to get her troubles from the same man. But, baby-making and having one was shrouded with so much mystery and fear that I did not entertain such thoughts for long.

During the whole period of confinement, Mmadira, like all the other new mothers I had seen, was cared for and pampered in many other ways as well. Relatives came bringing presents of chickens, eggs and other delicacies, all aimed at fattening her so that she would produce more milk for the baby. Our mother

hour, Noka and I were over at our uncle's place.
water for Lesego's bath and Noka was chopping
ing the water. Later more cousins came to hold the
mp sorghum for Lesego's dinner. Lesego, who was
e Mmadira, had, like Mmadira, to be washed,
fed regularly to ensure that she got her strength back
allenges of motherhood.

s we went about helping, there was an undercurrent
as my uncle, Rra-Gopane, had had other news as
g news, indeed.

I come with other news as well. Not happy news.'
ad finished drinking tea and was busy rolling a
: me some fire, little Nei,' he had requested. I had
ging a small smouldering piece of firewood for him
arette.

na-Monei had waited patiently, but when her brother
dly on his cigarette, frowning pensively, she could
tly. 'What is it, my brother? Don't keep me waiting.
g me.'

ne to invite you to our compound to discuss a very
indeed. It involves my son, Gopane.' My cousin
een killed by unknown assailants two years before.
lice had a new lead on who had done it.

y brother,' the sister urged. We all knew that her
en the news of the death of his only son very badly

e would still not look up into his sister's face. 'Yes,
that he was attacked by *tsotsis,* street rascals. The
e never caught, but it had always been assumed, by
east, that the gang was after his money. Well, now
ave come from Rhodesia and they say it was their
my son.'

ere does Rhodesia fit in? And why would they come
on't understand my brother. What are you saying?'
nfusion on her face. Even I paused from my pre-
traba game to look up in alarm. Rra-Gopane looked
is sister, his eyes wet with emotion. 'Their son, they
ith my son Gopane, at Western Deep Levels Mine.

showed her how to bathe the baby and washed the baby's napkins
as Mmadira lay next to her baby. Mmadira was given designated
eating utensils and only our mother or us young children could eat
any leftovers. She spent the three months sleeping, eating and
nursing the baby.

My sister was a mother of a white baby and a healer, two things
that set her apart from her age mates. She might not have been
married, but she had these two unique facts going for her. It
seemed to me that, once she stopped crying, she became an old
woman, full of wisdom and self-assuredness, almost overnight.
She threw herself into motherhood and healing with a zest and
enthusiasm that I had not been aware she possessed. I was proud
of her and took her baby with me almost everywhere I went.

CHAPTER 11

A few weeks after the birth of Dutchgirl, Rra-Gopane, my uncle, paid the family an early morning visit.

'Good morning, my sister,' he greeted my mother. I liked Rra-Gopane for his gentle manner. I moved away from him though because he was always grabbing us to tickle and being tickled always made me want to bite. And I had started to consider myself too old to be tickled like a child but he had not caught on yet.

'Good morning, my brother,' my mother responded. 'How are your children?'

'My children are well. Their mother is well. I'm well, but then the tongue lies about the health of the body. But the new baby thrives. How are your children?' Rra-Gopane seemed rather serious to me and he did not seem to be interested in grabbing me for a playful tickle. This set off alarm bells in my head so I stuck around to listen.

'My children are well, Rra-Gopane. Dutchgirl had a small minor problem. Her fontanel collapsed just a little bit. But I was able to take care of that. I have to say I was not sure whether a white baby could be treated successfully with traditional herbs. I have never had to treat a child who does not have a totem; it concerned me a great deal. But all is well, son of my father. All is well. Dutchgirl is feeding well once more. Nei, as you can see, is growing into a beautiful young lady. Noka has gone for firewood. Keneilwe is still unmarried and you know where my eye is looking on that matter. But a mother can only hope and be patient. It is not too late yet. And Leruo sends greetings from the City of Gold. His wife has been rude and discourteous some people say, clearly a

sign of early pregnancy. A m
brother.'

There was a pause as I ser
was obvious that he had somet
he brought the matter up. 'M
plaint from my wife. It's not a

My mother set her cup bacl
ground. A bit of tea spilled ont
ants to death.

'Oh, my brother, I was n
rubbing between me and your v
Mma-Sego next door? After all

'No, no, my sister. No, Mn
one. It is a small one. And you
wife, Mma-Gopane, is compla
your house to help you with M
they do not come to help my wi
confinement. It is not your faul
be mentioned. It is better to sto
mend it.' Rra-Gopane looked do

'I understand my brother. I u
ren think of Dutchgirl as some s
help and to hold her. You are rig
will send some of them to your
thought about it before.'

My uncle Fifi sipped from
I said, it is a small matter, my s
be mentioned, otherwise they wi

'You are correct, my brothei
your belly must be killed, but ev
you smash your own belly. It i
smash with aggression.' My n
matter was a small one. She was
with all relatives and to avoid qu

'Well spoken, my sister. Well
small matter. Yes, may the mon
monkey eat resin.'

'Yes, my brother, let there be

Within a
I was hewir
wood for he
baby and to
a *motsetse*
massaged ar
to meet the

But even
in the famil
well. Distur

'My sist
Rra-Gopane
cigarette. 'C
complied, b
to light his

At first,
sucked repe
not wait pat
You are sca

'I have
grave matt
Gopane ha
Perhaps the

'Go on,
brother had
indeed.

Rra-Go
you will re
assailants
the police
some peop
son who ki

'What?
to tell you'
There was
tended *mo*
up and fac
say, worke

And he killed him over a woman, not money. So they now come into my house, speaking a foreign tongue and they want to give me a young girl as compensation for my son!'

'What? I have never heard such a tale before! Just as our hearts were getting healed these crazy people come with this story! I swear by my father, who bore me, I have never heard such a tale!'

'They say it is their tradition.'

'What? To kill other people's sons?' My mother was agitated and perhaps frightened.

'Just listen my sister. My heart is heavy with confusion. Two men are at my house as I speak.'

'You mean you were busy telling me about your wife's complaint about a minor matter while this was hanging over your heart? You mean…' My mother had raised her voice and a chicken that was pecking next to her flew off in fright.

'Listen, my sister. My heart is heavy, and you know when I am like that, I have to find distractions. These men are the emissaries for their family, they say. The rest will come tomorrow. What should I tell them? Should I give their son to the police? And which police? This happened in South Africa, two years ago. These police here will say it is not their case. Or should I go to Rhodesia to report the matter? I don't even know the road to Rhodesia! This is not an easy matter! And these men are saying it is their custom to pay compensation in cases such as this. They say the girl is young and a virgin and can give me more children. Perhaps she will bear me sons, they say. They are a family of many sons, they tell me.'

'My brother, this is not your case alone. You must tell the men from Rhodesia to go away. We must meet as the Kgang family to discuss this matter. This is not an easy matter. Yes, I say this is not your case alone.'

'You know I have no son now. I have seven girls and no hope of having any more sons. When Lesego was expecting, I thought perhaps I would have a grandson. But I didn't. Perhaps this is …'

'My brother, I say this is not an easy matter. Don't let your heavy heart fly away with dreams. You can't decide it so easily. It is not our culture to accept compensation for a dead member of the family. And who is this girl? How old is she? How can you even

97

think of taking her as your woman or concubine or whatever? What kind of children will a Rhodesian have?'

'Well, you know the saying: all women are just women, only the man carries the totem. So who this girl is is not very important. And look at Dutchgirl. Isn't she bringing you joy, although she is of some strange combination?'

'Don't try to get away from the real issue here. I say tell the Rhodesians to come back in a month. I say you call a family meeting so that this matter can be discussed. Don't make any promises to the Rhodesians. In fact, threaten them. How can you look the killers of your own son in the face and even consider marrying one of their own? And they can't be very nice people! They kill and they even offer their own flesh and blood as payment! I am so happy I am not a Rhodesian! What tribe in Rhodesia are these people anyway?'

Rra-Gopane's head was bowed as he said, 'I hear what you are saying, my sister. And you are right. But I have not told you the whole story. They say their son is now mad, as a result of shedding innocent blood. They say the only way for him to be cured is if we forgive him and we accept the girl as compensation. They don't care whether or not we tell the police. They just want forgiveness so that their son will get some relief. My son is tormenting him, demanding that he own up to what he did. So accepting their offer will also mean my son's spirit will rest in peace.'

'Oh, Bakgatla who bore me! Wasn't it this past ploughing season that I told you that Gopane was restless? Now you tell me the reason why? I have seen him in my dreams! He wails, "let me go, let me go!" I told you he was restless and now you tell me the reason why! Oh my brother, I say tell the men to go back. Tell the Rhodesians to go back. This is a serious matter indeed! It can't be decided easily. And Mma-Gopane will have to say her piece! Gopane was her son too and you are her husband! Her people will have to be involved.'

'You don't think we have to act fast? Like now?'

'No. I say you call at our uncle's house and brief him, and the two of you go over and politely tell the men from Rhodesia that you have heard them but the family needs to meet first before a final decision is made. And don't offer them room in your house.

It would not be a good thing to do. Ask a neighbour to put them up for the night. And don't make any promises. They want to cure their son. You want your son's spirit to rest in peace. They have their culture. We have our own. We have to think carefully about this matter, my brother.'

'Thank you, my sister. I came to you first because, even though you are not a man, you have a good head. Do you want to meet the men? The emissaries, I mean?'

'Not to discuss this weighty matter, but I do want to see them. Just with my two eyes. I want to see these people, who will give their child away to strangers. No, not to hear their story. Just for you to tell them, "this is my sister, she has come to help my wife with our daughter who has a new baby" and to tell me "these are guests from a distant land." We must be cautious. It mustn't be said later that you took a woman to meet men on such an important matter, before you told all the men in our family. I will pretend that I have come to see *motsetse* and the baby.'

'You are right, my sister.'

'I forgot to ask, what language do they speak? They can't speak Setswana surely?'

'One of them speaks a bit of Setswana. But mainly they speak Fanagalo, the language of the mines.'

'Oh, of course, you understand that. Next time, they must bring a good interpreter. Tell them that. And you will need Rra-Sera. Nothing can be decided without him, so you will have to go to the Chief to seek special permission for him to be allowed into the village. His year's banishment to the cattle post is almost over anyway, so the Chief should be sympathetic. Perhaps the Chief too must be told about the Rhodesians and their request.'

'That Rra-Sera, I wish he would stop this constant battle with the Chief! This is the second time he got himself banished from the village.'

'That is not the important thing right now. And I dare say, even though I am just a woman, that Rra-Sera was right this last time! The Chief was way out of line.'

'Don't let anyone hear you say that!'

My mother snorted, 'Am I shouting it out to the world? Am I not speaking to my brother in my house?'

'Let me go, my sister. I will see you later over at my compound. Thank you for all your suggestions.'

'Go well, my brother. May our ancestors guide you on this one.'

'Stay well, daughter of my father.'

After that I would dream about the Rhodesian girl, whom I named Nozipho, because that was the only Rhodesian name I knew. In my dreams, Nozipho eloped with a boy in her class and they went to live on a mountain, surrounded by a garden of wild berries, birds and wild animals. The Nozipho of my dreams was extremely happy. During the daytime though, when I thought of Nozipho, I was filled with fear. What if there was a similar custom amongst the Bakgatla? I certainly did not know all the customs and traditions.

Then, one day, Berka Solomon wrote me a letter in which he declared that, 'Time and opportunity has moved my emotions with trepidation to pen this humble transcription of love to you and transmit the hope that deep affections are mutually enjoyed and interchanged. Last night, I was perambulating in the geographical vicinity of your yard, stars above my head, dreaming of circumambulating you. Please accept my humble declaration of love.' This was my first love letter so I was extremely happy, although I didn't understand the whole of it. Mary had received at least two love letters and I had been very jealous. I showed Mary the letter and she was certain that Berka Solomon had copied a letter his older sister had received from a secondary school student known for his big words. The older boy, Mary said, was in the school debating team. It was obvious to me that Mary was just being jealous. Berka Solomon had always been good with the Queen's language. Everyone knew that. Mary argued, 'Why then is the letter full of so many cancellations?' I replied, 'Because he was thinking out what he had to say to me carefully.' After that, I didn't speak to Mary for two full days but she came to apologise and admitted that she had been jealous. She did say though that she didn't think I should let Berka Solomon circumambulate me. I too was bit concerned about his wanting to do that, especially because we could not find the word in the class dictionary.

I didn't respond to Berka Solomon's letter, but just knowing that there was someone to elope with, should it look like I needed an out, was very comforting. It did bother me though that it was said that Berka Solomon's mother, before she died and as she was in the process of giving birth to Berka Solomon, had been transfused with white man's blood. I imagined her heart pumping the white man's blood through her body and into the then-being-born Berka Solomon. No doubt the white man's blood accounted for Berka Solomon's impressive command of the Queen's language and that was something to be proud of. But, after my past association with Mosweu, marrying Berka Solomon would bring me even closer to having an albino child. But then running off and marrying a boy with white man's blood coursing through his veins, who spoke the Queen's language, was infinitely better than being given away to strangers. And surely Dutchgirl's existence was evidence enough that black blood and white blood could mix just fine?

It worried me a little bit that I had promised Kabo that I would not marry anyone else although it was long before this Rhodesian affair and surely I could be forgiven? I did worry a lot about Nozipho though, and hoped she did elope in real life.

CHAPTER 12

Rra-Sera, my uncle whom the Chief had banished from the village for a year on two occasions, was a very cantankerous character. When my parents spoke about him, it was with both exasperation and admiration. During a drought year, when cattle were lean and few, his daughter Sametsi, Sera's older sister, was married to Lelang Mokibe, a man related, albeit distantly, to the Chief. Two lean cattle had been paid as *bogadi*. Rra-Sera had always had great plans for the wedding of his first daughter so he had suggested a postponement for a year or two, hoping that the earth would be recharged and the cattle might become more plentiful and attractive. The groom's family had been insistent. Their last daughter had been married the year before so they needed a young woman to help with domestic chores. The groom's mother was eager for some help, her knees were beginning to give and her back was feeling its age. So the wedding had taken place, thin cattle and all.

Four years and two children later, my cousin Sametsi had fallen ill. Her husband was at the mines in South Africa. On a visit to see her daughter, my aunt Mma-Sera had been shocked by her condition. She was clearly suffering from *boswagadi,* brought on by a sexual encounter with an unclean widow or widower. Mma-Sera trusted her daughter, so the only possibility was that Sametsi's husband was the one at fault. There were stories of women of questionable repute hanging around mine hostels in Johannesburg. Fast, scheming women who could trick the most faithful of husbands. They were after money and the men, segregated in dormitory-like residences called hostels, and lonely for female company, were easy prey. But not only was Sametsi sick, her mother-in-law was demanding that she continue with her domestic chores. As if that was not enough, there appeared to be no plans to call Sametsi's husband home for curing. No doctor had been identified for the curing.

Urgent and furious consultations were made amongst Sametsi's family and a delegation was sent to Sametsi's in-laws.

'We have come to inquire about the health of your daughter,' Sametsi's uncle had started off, after the polite enough exchange of greetings. Sametsi was her in-law's daughter since she had been married off and cattle, though lean and sorry-looking, had been paid as *bogadi*. The politeness had not lasted long. Soon the bitterness Sametsi's parents felt at what they saw as their daughter's ill-treatment erupted to the surface. There was much finger pointing and raised voices.

'You may have paid two miserable and sickly cows for her, but I bore her. It was my womb that carried her and my breasts that fed her! She is my daughter and she is coming home with us,' Sametsi's mother hissed at her daughter's mother-in-law.

'Are you engineering the divorce of your own daughter? The whole village will know that, amongst your family, a divorcee resides!' Sametsi's mother-in-law was well aware of the stigma of divorce and she was challenging the other side to say the dreaded words.

'Divorce is better than death, I say!' Rra-Sera's father had answered.

The uncles on both sides had done their best to calm the respective parents.

Finally, after hours of discussion, during which Sametsi's family had turned down offered food and water and had made it clear that something urgent had to be done to address the problem at hand, it was decided that Sametsi would go with her own family to recuperate. This had been a major concession by her in-laws. A married woman did not go back to her parents' home except under very special circumstances. She particularly did not go back when sick. The agreement though, was that Sametsi would be returned when her husband came back for *boswagadi* treatment. It was agreed that a letter would be written to the mine bosses, informing them of urgent business back in Botswana, requiring the attendance of Lelang Mokibe. Perhaps the death of a very close family member would have to be claimed.

Rra-Sera however had other plans. Not only did he secure a traditional doctor to treat his daughter, but he also dramatised the end of the marriage in a way that would be talked about for years to come. Three months after taking away his daughter, the Mokibe family woke up to find two pathetic-looking cattle tied to two supporting poles of their main rondavel. The cattle were so thin that they could hardly stand.

The Mokibe family was incensed by what they considered, and which indeed was intended to be, an insult. They reported the matter to the Chief who called both sets of families.

It turned out that Rra-Sera had deliberately starved the animals and this, the Chief said, was cruel. Rra-Sera had little respect for the Chief and his contempt was obvious from the way he answered him. He was only giving back to Mokibe what he had received unless, of course, the Chief thought the cattle were too fat, in which case he could have that dealt with. His daughter, unlike some others who were sold at exorbitant prices, was not for sale. One of the headmen in attendance had just married off a daughter to a man from the Bakwena tribe. Although, according to Bakgatla custom, a family did not negotiate the number of cattle but simply accepted what was offered, it was believed that the *bogadi* of fourteen cattle had been negotiated. So the barb about the sale of daughters was obviously in reference to that. When the Chief ruled that the marriage had not been properly terminated and that the families should go back and go through the proper steps for such termination, Rra-Sera had stood up and left, his family in tow. He was a tall man who walked with a swagger and the gun he was carrying over his shoulder added authority to his bearing.

A few minutes later, while the Chief was still considering how to punish Rra-Sera for his disrespect, a gun shot and then another shattered the morning calm. When the Chief and a whole crowd of people assembled at the house of Mokibe to find out what had happened, the two cows were still tied to the two poles, only they were dead and bleeding. Rra-Sera had left after declaring that he no longer had a relationship with the Mokibes.

At first, the Chief had demanded that Rra-Sera collect the cows, but Rra-Sera had told the messengers that it was not his duty to clean up after the Mokibe family or after their relatives. That was when the Chief banished him to the cattle post for the second time in four years.

The first time he had been banished was after his father had died, leaving in his care, not only the family cattle, but also a herd of ten cattle belonging to the Chief's family. Rra-Sera's family had, like few other families in the village, been entrusted with herding cattle for the Chief. Every year they had to care for the cattle and help plough one of many fields owned by the Chief and his family. Rra-Sera had decided that he would not be inheriting his father's role as a *lelata* or Chief's servant, so he had driven the cattle to the *kgotla* kraal one morning and then waited for the Chief to arrive. He had calmly informed him of his decision and then left.

In both cases Rra-Sera's response to the order of banishment had been to slaughter a goat and make a feast before packing his family, including those in school, off to the cattle post. When he came back, his wife brewed beer and he slaughtered a cow and he made another feast. Those who came to feast with him did so out of curiosity, but had been nervous that the Chief might think they were disrespectful of his decision. Still, it was always difficult to keep away from free meat and beer, so family members and neighbours came.

At *kgotla* meetings, Rra-Sera was one of the main participants, asking questions and making suggestions. He would demand explanations about why schools did not close in the winter to allow children to be at home. He would suggest that community projects, like building of dams and schools, be assigned to specific regiments. The Chief always found a way of crediting Rra-Sera's suggestions to himself.

My father was always trying to help Rra-Sera to get off the perpetual collision course with the Chief. 'Do you have to ram your head at a rock, Rra-Sera?' Rra-Sera's retort was almost always, 'I refuse to let any man tell me how to live.' He vowed the next time he tried to banish him, he would refuse. 'Let him try once again,' he declared, 'and you will see a daylight ghost. You will see the buttocks of a baboon. Mark my words, you will see very ugly things!'

My father never did see the threatened ugly things, for the Chief never banished my uncle again. As the two feuding men grew older, their animosity towards each other simmered to occasional angry spats. They may even have grudgingly respected each other.

CHAPTER 13

The day my father arrived from the cattle post, after the three months of silence over the birth of Dutchgirl, was a particularly hot one. It was so hot that one could quite literally hear the sun drying up the earth. Sun crickets crackled and the air stood still. When we spotted the slim figure struggling against fatigue, the sand and the sun, we all fell silent. The silence that had hung around him as he left came back with him and we could feel it thicken around us as he came closer. My mother stood up and went into one of the rondavels to bring her husband's chair. It had not been used for three months, so spiders and a wasp had made their homes on it, looping cobwebs around the leather strings. My mother quickly brushed the homes off with a grass broom. Then she went and got a jug of water. Then she went to get a bowl of food, sour sorghum porridge with chicken and gravy. It was a Sunday and a chicken had been killed for lunch. My mother had dished out for him as she had done at every meal in the past six months. She had expected that we, the children, would have the food as an afternoon snack as she had not received any word about his return.

My father walked into the yard, pushing the silence against the cluster that was us, his family, sitting under the *mosetlha* tree. He was the one arriving, so he had to offer the greetings, but what if he did not? Dutchgirl had been lying on her back, offering funny giggly sounds to all, but her mother, Mmadira, snatched her up and planted her protectively on her lap.

'*Dumelang*,' my father said, stabbing at the silence. He sat down, took off his battered hat and placed it over his left knee.

His face was glistening with sweat. He looked leaner than I remembered him. And older too.

'*Dumela* Rra-Leruo,' my mother responded, calling her husband by their oldest child. She extended her right hand to her husband, bowing slightly to show respect.

'Are the children well?' my father asked, taking his wife's hand in both of his. A sign of peace. I heard a sigh of relief ripple through the small group and I relaxed also.

The greetings over, my mother scooped a gourd-full of water from a bucket set under the tree for cooling. 'You must be tired, here is some water to drink. And yes, the children are well, father of my children.'

My father took the offered gourd and used a bit of the water to wash his hot sweaty face. He then drank deeply, almost hungrily. He then stood up and put the gourd to Dutchgirl's mouth. The child latched on and gulped eagerly. 'You should not keep children thirsty like this,' he rebuked lightly. 'It's a hot day. Children need lots of water. And Monei, aren't you going to come and say *dumela* to your father? Come, my child.' With that, the silence was broken.

The following day, my father selected a fat goat and had it killed to celebrate *mantsho,* the coming out of confinement, albeit a week late, of baby Dutchgirl. He also gave the baby a new name, Ewetse, meaning 'the heart has settled', to announce the happiness and gratitude he felt for the arrival of one more life in his family.

After that my father could be seen feeding, carrying and tickling the little girl. A thing he had never done with any of his own children.

It was towards the end of the day of the *mantsho* ceremony that Monei's mother told her husband about the visit from her brother.

'I have heard of that custom. But it is not our custom. But then it is not for me to decide. Your family will have to decide the matter.'

'I agree with you. And I keep on thinking of Monei and wondering whether, if this were my custom, I could give her up to cure Noka's madness. I don't think that I could. And I cannot imagine that she would go willingly!'

'Perhaps, growing up in Rhodesia, little girls know that they might be given away as compensation in this way. So perhaps it is not such a shock.'

'It has to be a shock, Rra-Leruo! It has to be! This girl must be sixteen or younger! She cannot expect that her brother will go off to the mines, kill someone, go mad with guilt! I wouldn't do it, even if it were my culture.'

'Yes, you are correct my wife. Knowing that a practice exists, and actually being dispatched to some distant place as payment for something you did not do, in accordance with that custom, has to be two different things. I am happy it is not our culture. These are hard matters. Hard matters, indeed. When is your family meeting? I can only attend and make suggestions, since I am only an in-law. But I say don't accept this young girl. Your ancestors would not be pleased, I tell you! Now you know why Gopane's spirit was restless. Deal with that our way! Don't go inviting bigger problems by doing things in accordance with some strange and foreign custom. And don't trust your brother's views on this one. The idea of some young second wife for whom he has paid no cattle may well be clouding his mind. What does he say, anyway?'

'He is leaving the decision to the family.' My mother did not want to admit to her husband that her brother's mind was already clouded.

'That's good. Not many men would say "no thank you" to this kind of offer very easily. But then, I can't see how any man could live with the sister of the killer of his son! It is madness! Pure madness! I swear by my father, who is lying at Ranko's cemetery, this is pure madness. You just have to think about it for only a minute to realise that to accept the compensation would be the beginning of disaster!'

'I agree with you, Rra-Leruo. I agree.'

My father was silent for a while before saying, 'There is another matter I must tell you about. Rradipotsane has sprung a third leg on the matter we discussed last year. He will not give us two heifers as we agreed. I am going to have to report the matter to the headman for a decision. That man can not be trusted!'

'How can he hope to get away with this? There are witnesses that he shot and killed our bull! There are witnesses that he agreed to pay two heifers as compensation! I was never convinced that two heifers were sufficient compensation for that bull, but now he won't even do that! What's his excuse? That son of morally deficient ancestors!'

'Now he is saying he shot the bull because it had a broken leg. He was doing us a favour he says. Otherwise the bull would have died in the bush and been vulture meat. I asked him why then did he eat the meat; if he was doing us a favour, he would have dried the meat and sent word to us about what had happened.'

'What is his answer to that question?'

'He says he did not eat the meat. He claims dogs went into his hut and ate the meat. I tell you, I have never met a more infuriating scoundrel. Indeed a snake can only sire a snake! That was exactly how his father was. He told you the sun rose from the East and you started wondering about even that. Only last year, his sister was returned by her in-laws! Returned on a clear day, for taking up with her husband's cowherder and for drunkenness. I cannot imagine an insult worse than a woman taking up with her husband's employee! The most foul-mouthed, sneaky woman who ever walked this earth. You would think with that scandal still in the minds of everyone, they would at least pretend to be honourable! A family of scoundrels, they are. Our misfortune to get mixed up with them.'

'But Rra-Leruo, this will have to wait until after this Rhodesian affair, won't it? We don't want to give Rradipotsane time to concoct another story but we have this pressing matter to meet over. Don't you agree?'

'You are right, mother of my children. What is a bull compared to a matter that could make all your ancestors rise up in anger? Yes, this matter will have to wait until after the harvest is in. But it makes me furious even to think about it. That man is so dishonest he can steal milk from a cup of tea even as you lift it to your mouth!'

CHAPTER 14

My grandmother, Mma-Tsietsi, was always full of sayings. 'You can't wash a name like you would a piece of cloth, child of my child. The stain on a name goes much deeper. It stains the heart. How can you wash a soiled heart? You can't, my child. You can't.' This she would say whenever anyone made a disparaging remark about another. I was always asking her to tell me a story or to explain some mysterious expression I had overheard. I think although she pretended to be exasperated by my questions, she secretly enjoyed telling me things no one else would.

'*Nkoko*, tell me about *thotse*,' I implored my grandmother. 'What does it mean to bite *thotse*?' My grandmother laughed her throaty laugh, but immediately covered her mouth and whispered, 'Oh, child of my child! You ask such impossible questions! These are matters way older than you are! These are not matters for young heads! Where did you even hear about that?'

'I overheard uncle Rra-Lesego saying he wants to be home until after the end of fertility month, December, so he can bite *thotse*. He was telling his friend Rra-Kabo and when I asked what they were talking about they chased me away, calling me big ears! Will you tell me?'

'And if your mother catches me telling you these things she will be very angry!'

'Can you tell me tonight, when I help you with your bath? Will you, *Nkoko*?'

'Only if you promise not to repeat what I tell you to anyone. Do you promise?'

'I promise! I promise! Here, I have threaded your needle. Can

111

I thread the other one as well? I want to go off to play at Nawa Ward. We are playing *koi* against girls from that ward.'

'That's fine, my grandchild. I have enough thread here to mend this hem. Don't forget to come back in time to heat my bath water.'

'And miss the story?'

'Lower your voice! You will get me into trouble with your mother at this rate!'

I loved helping my grandmother with her baths, not only because I got her to tell me secret things, but also because I loved the feel of her flesh. It felt loose, like it was not attached to the bones underneath. First I would wet the old woman's back, then gently scrub it with a piece of stone, smoothing the flesh and rubbing off dead skin. I would then lather her smooth skin, running my hand up and down her back playfully, until I finally rinsed her off. I always wanted to prolong these weekly intimacies and, especially in winter, I always heated an extra bucket of water. I did not mind having to haul the water for, the longer I stayed with my grandmother, the more stories she told me. Sometimes, my grandmother would lie on her tummy and I would massage her back with suds, kneading special areas as requested by the old woman. Once I was done, I would leave her to finish her washing and dressing, but I would always come back later to clean up after her. Then I would hang out her clothes, always a blouse, a skirt and two petticoats, which she would have washed. Like other old women her age, she wore two petticoats as under-garments, and nothing else.

I must have been about eleven when my great aunt Naniso died. For weeks, my grandmother could not be coaxed into telling a story or prolonging her baths. I found it strange how the two old women, though not related by blood, seemed to share some deep bond. Even my father was sadder than one would expect a man to be at the loss of an aunt. For weeks my grandmother did not sing as she mended clothes or made *makgabe* for her grandchildren. She no longer declared happily, as she used to, 'My heart is full of stories, my grandchildren. Do you want to hear a story from my heart?' Her heart seemed to be filled with sorrow, instead. I was afraid she would never tell me stories and secrets again but she did come around and the day she promised to tell me what biting *thotse* meant I had heated an extra bucket of water to prolong our private time together.

'The water won't get cold, grandmother, I have an extra bucket of hot water right here. Tell me the story of the key around your waist. Will you? You have promised to tell me that story.' I had decided that the meaning of *thotse* could wait for another occasion. She still seemed sad so I thought a story about her life would cheer both of us up.

'Nei, I have told you that story many times. In fact, I have an idea. Why don't you tell me the story? Let's hear if you have been listening to me all this time.'

'Grandmother, that is not fair. How can I possibly tell your story? I can't tell it right.'

'One day you will have to tell all these stories to your own children. This will give you practice. So tell me about the key and if you tell the story well, I will open that chest on a Saturday when you have no school and I will show you what is in there.'

I scooped handfuls of warm water and ran it over her back and began, 'My grandmother had a brown key around her waist...'

'No, Nei, you must start at the beginning.

'Let me start again, *Nkoko*. My grandmother was a beautiful young woman. Her name was Lelegaisang, meaning, the greatest love of all. And yes, she was loved all her life. First by her family and then later by a most beautiful man. And later by her children and yet even later by her grandchildren. She was, in turn, full of love.

'As a young woman ready for marriage, she had the walk of a mature woman. Her hips swung as she walked and her back was straight. Oh, you should have seen her when she had a claypot on her head. Her back straight, her shoulders like a beam over a doorway.' I paused and asked, 'Am I telling it right grandmother?'

'Yes, child of my child. Imagine that you are bathing your own child. She is six years old, and she has never met me. I was gone long before she was born. What would you tell her? And remember, it is a long story that cannot be told at one sitting. You must not rush it, or she will not take it seriously.'

'Her breasts thrust forward. And her hair was in tiny little coils. Not like these days, when every one is using the white man's comb to mix up their hair, sometimes even using a hot iron to straighten it. No, not like these days. She was the colour of a *moretlwa* switch and she needed no skin lightening creams to improve her complexion. Her complexion needed no improving at all. In any event, she was a beauty long before the advent of skin lightening creams.

'Even before her initiation into womanhood, many men had noticed her. In fact, when she was only a young girl, fathers were already pointing her out to their sons. But that is not how she chose her future husband! It was not at the watering hole or while out collecting firewood. It was not even at the annual singing competitions!

'This is how it happened. She was an only girl amongst six boys. So she did not have to do any of the male tasks. She never had to watch goats or milk them. But her uncle gave her a goat she loved and when it had a kid she loved that little kid so much that she would be seen in the ward carrying it. One day the kid did not come home with the rest of the herd. She went out looking for it. Coming back, with the kid in her arms, she stepped on a thorn that went right through her foot. A young man out looking for his family goats heard her screams. Whistling to let her know that help was on the way, he ran through the bush towards her. What he saw was a beautiful young woman, with tears streaming down her cheeks, clutching a scared little goat. She was hobbling along the path.'

'That is enough for today Nei. Let me finish up washing. Just remember where you are with the story next time. You are good little storyteller! Your grandchildren will love you for it. And, of course, worry you endlessly as well!' My grandmother was laughing a little. A thing she had not done for a while. I was proud that I had brought that on.

Over the next six weeks, I retold the story of my grandmother. I recounted how the young man had gently removed the thorn from my grandmother's foot. How he had prised the kid from her arms, encouraged it to follow them, and carried the young girl into the village on his back. The young girl's naked breasts seemed to melt into the young man's naked back. The boy and the girl were silent, and both were keenly aware of the beating of their hearts. And how upon reaching my grandmother's compound, the young man had boldly pronounced to my great-grandparents, 'Greetings, my elders. My name is Mfafu. I am the son of Mosu and Pelonomi of Mosibudula Ward. Mosu, who is the son of Borekhu. Mosu the Brave, of the Maunatlala Regiment. Borekhu, who dug a well at Tauteng during the three year drought. And, my elders, I believe I have found my wife.'

Everyone laughed good-naturedly, thanked the young man and told him to pass on their greetings to his own parents. When the young man put on a solemn face and declared that he was serious, my great-grandmother had replied jokingly, 'A wife is not picked up in the bush like firewood, my son! We thank you for bringing our daughter home, but I do believe you have your family goats to take home? It's getting dark. They will go astray if you don't go after them. And who knows! You might find yourself another wife! They seem to be everywhere. Perhaps falling from the sky?'

'Was that confidence or arrogance we just saw, I wonder?' My great-grandmother was not sure whether to be offended or amused.

'A lot of both, I would say! A lot of both!' my great-grandfather was still chuckling.

My grandmother was always the one to tell me to stop. I was so enchanted with the story of her courtship and marriage that I could happily tell it till the sun came up.

But, even before I had retold the whole story to her, my grandmother one morning failed to wake up. She had died in her sleep.

The agreement had been that she would open the chest upon my finishing the story but one Saturday morning, which turned out to be five weeks before she died, she decided that it was time.

'Nei, child of my child, come, I have something to show you. It's time to open the chest.' There was both happiness and sadness in her voice. I would later decide that she had known she was about to die. At the time though, I hopped with excitement as I followed her into the rondavel we shared with Noka. I was very happy no one was around to interfere with my special time with my grandmother. Although I had long established the right to sleep closest to my grandmother at night, Noka would sometimes try to unseat me. Finally, my grandmother had each one of us sleep on either side of her.

As we approached the wooden chest, the sun was low on the

115

western horizon and a shaft of light streamed through the small window of the rondavel, falling directly on the chest. My grandmother reached under her two petticoats and unfastened a strip of flannel cloth, which, as far as I could remember, had always been fastened around her waist. Tied to the strip was a small bronze-coloured key.

My grandmother, I noticed, had oiled the little padlock hanging from the front of the chest. I remembered that five days earlier, she had asked my father for some grease, but I had not thought much about her need for that.

'Nei, I haven't seen the contents of this chest in years! So I'm as excited as you are. Oh, this brings memories, Nei! Wonderful memories. Some sad though. But mainly wonderful! Your grandfather was such a special person. I wish for you a man as full of love and compassion as my husband was. May the ancestors bless you and give you such a man. And child of my child, please bring a gourd of *morula* wine from the pot outside. This calls for a celebration and what else to do it with than with *morula* wine, your grandfather's favourite brew?'

I didn't trust my voice so I didn't respond. I thought I might squeak like a cricket if I opened my mouth. I quietly went out of the house and returned shortly with a gourd full of *morula* wine. The clear liquid had a sweet smell and I could restrain myself from having a sip before my grandmother – an act that would have been a sign of disrespect. I handed her the gourd and she tilted it and let a small amount spill onto the earth floor for the ancestors. She closed her eyes for a few seconds, no doubt talking with her husband through her heart. She took a deep sip and handed the gourd back to me and I did the same, tasting the cool sweet-smelling wine. I had always loved *morula* wine and I also knew that in a day's time I would not be allowed to drink, since it would have fermented further, its alcoholic content rising as a result. I set the gourd aside and sat down to watch as my grandmother inserted and turned the key and the padlock sprang open with ease. I don't know what I was expecting but I could hardly breathe. The chest had been in that one place, with padlock rusted and ignored, for as long as I could remember.

'Come Nei. Come closer. In fact, pull down those pillows so we can sit. Let's relax and dream of the past. Go back to the past with me, so you can take the past to the future.'

I made two sets of pillow piles for my grandmother and me, and together, like two co-conspirators, we lifted the lid of the chest, and the hinges squeaked from years of not being worked. My first reaction was to rear back but I was happy to note that my grandmother had done the same thing. Neither of us had expected the powerful smell of mothballs that hit us. But our single-mindedness brought our heads back to the chest, eyes peering into the semi-darkness. Then she took out the items one by one.

The first was a skirt made of soft brown leather and decorated with beads and bird feathers, though all that remained of the feathers were tiny stocks. The mothballs had not completely protected the more delicate part of the feathers from disintegration. I was momentarily confused. The skirt was too skimpy for my grandmother, who wore ankle length skirts with two sets of petticoats underneath. The skimpy skirt could not possibly fit around my grandmother's waist, let alone accommodate two flannel skirts underneath it. I had never seen a garment like that, except in a book at the library.

'Oh, Nei, I was the slimmest young girl. But I tell you after just one pregnancy, I was a true woman.' My grandmother held the dress to her chest and started laughing. 'Your grandfather made this skirt for me when we were courting. I laugh because he made it for the girl he fell in love with, but once we were married I could not wear it any more. It's a girl's skirt. And, of course, after our first child I couldn't possibly fit into it. His family was so taken with me! Feeding me and fattening me. I tell you by the time I left confinement after three months, three goats and countless chickens had been slaughtered. '*Mma,* you will spoil her!' my husband used to mock-scold her mother for loving me so much! I was full-figured and beautiful. My skin was as smooth as a baby's from being massaged and protected from the sun. Still, I would look at this skirt and miss the days of our courting, when I was a beautiful girl with a waist as slim as a grass broom.'

I kept quiet for a while, giving my grandmother time with her thoughts. It seemed almost like she was talking to herself. Finally I asked, '*Nkoko* can I touch it? Feel it?'

'Of course, of course. Here.' The skin was soft and the sewing delicate. And the beads were exquisite. A lot of love and care had gone into making the little garment. Then my grandmother suggested, 'Nei, child of my child, try it on.' She whispered the last part. I was seized with trepidation. Would the skirt fit? Did I have a waist as slim as a grass broom? Was my grandfather watching? What would he think? Would he be pleased?

'Grandmother, I can't,' I whispered back. 'I'm not beautiful like you were.'

'Oh Nei, why do you think you are my special grandchild? Hasn't your mother told you enough times that each heart has a match or, if you are lucky, matches? That each one of us has another with whom we will have a special bond? Why do you think your mother spends more time with Mmadira than with any other child? That I spend more time with you? It's not just about love. Of course, I love you. But so does your mother. And I do love all my grandchildren. But you are also my special heart-match. Our hearts have the same rhythm, Nei. Surely you know that? Right now, your grandfather, Mfafu is smiling watching us. Please put it on for me and for him.'

'But grandmother, I'm not beautiful like you were.'

'Nei, I can assure you that you are as beautiful as it is possible for any young woman to be. If your parents were not so good at putting the word out that you are not available for marriage, this yard would be a dust patch, from all the men and their parents trampling it. Now, Nei, beautiful Nei, will you make an old woman happy? Will you put on the skirt?'

I took off the dress I had on, removed the *makgabe* underneath and fastened the velvety skirt around my waist. It fitted perfectly and suddenly I did feel beautiful. Topless, I twirled around and my grandmother let out a hoot of laughter. I stopped, smiled at her and started to dance, although there was no music. Seeing this my grandmother reached for a drum that was nearby and started to beat it and sing at the same time. She sang about *molope,* a bird with feathers of all lengths and all colours. She asked the bird for a few feathers, so she too could be beautiful again. It was a song we had sung together before, so I sang with her.

'You have beauty in your heart, and beauty in your feathers,
Molope, lend me your feathers, so I can be beautiful.
Molope, wish me beauty in my heart, please my friend.
Molope, wish me beauty in my heart.'

At the end of the song, we laughed and hugged and cried. A few of the beads popped off, the threads giving up after years of storage.

'Let's see what else is in here, Nei, child of my child.' My grandmother reached into the chest and brought out a small little scarf and untied a knot that, at first, would not give. When it did yield, a gold earring was revealed. 'Oh, *Nkoko,* this is the other earring! All this time you thought it was lost!' My grandmother didn't respond at first. She regarded the earring in her palm and her eyes glistened with tears. Then, after what seemed like a very long time, she responded, 'Nei, child of my child. Here, put it on.' When I didn't respond she put the earring on my lap, and it rested there, amongst the beads and the withered feathers. The story of these earrings had been one of my favourite stories. I had imagined how this one had been lost and had wondered how something that had meant so much to two people could be rusted and ignored somewhere, without a trace. I had always assumed that it had fallen off her ear when she was out working in the fields or fixing the *lapa* walls or floors. Or doing some other routine work. When I was younger and before I had heard the story of the earrings, I had even asked for the one she always wore.

'*Nkoko,*' I had said, 'What use is one earring? Please give it to me. Then I can wear it as a finger ring. My fingers are slim enough.' The answer had been a definite 'No!'

Then one day, as I washed her back, she told me a story that was both funny and touching. Apparently, her husband Mfafu had taken a trip to Kimberly to buy a few items for the household. Kimberly was a long way to travel, but the train was reliable and safe and prices there were less exorbitant than those charged by local traders. He was particularly after a plough, two hoes, an axe and a large three-legged cast-iron pot. They needed a bigger plough, on account of the bigger field he had just cleared. The three-legged pot was for brewing beer and cooking at family gatherings like funerals, end of confinements and weddings. It was splurging, he knew, but a woman was not quite complete until she had her own big pot. Of course, she would have to borrow additional pots whenever there was a family gathering. That was expected, but it was also expected that a married woman would have at least one pot she could call her own. He had already been feeling that he had left it a bit too late. So off to Kimberly he went, expecting to be back within two weeks.

On his way back, he must have been singing in his heart, confident that his trip had been successful. He had all the items he had gone off to get and a little more: a secret he expected to keep until the very right moment. The train was on time and, as had been arranged, his brothers had come to meet him with his best span of twelve cattle pulling a wagon. His wife was there as well to meet him. On her lap was their two-year-old son, my father Tsietsi. My grandfather had issued requests to friends and relatives who had come to meet the train to help him offload his goods while he went to meet his wife and his son. When the offloading had been done, a congratulatory crowd had assembled around him and other returning travellers, and greetings had been exchanged with the travellers asking for the latest news. Just then, the train let out a hoot and started to move off. In response, and to everyone's amazement, my grandfather had pushed aside his wife who had been standing next to him, and ran towards the train. But when it became clear it had gathered too much speed, he had charged a man who was holding the reigns of his horse. Before, he had been talking to him rather amiably so, when he pushed him away and grabbed the reigns of the horse, everyone gasped with shock. Next thing they knew, he was galloping away. After some uncertainty, the party drove the span of cattle home. The horseman was given a ride and the brother offered his apologies to him, declaring that he could not imagine what had gotten into Mfafu's head. It was assumed that he must have forgotten something in the train, but still his single-mindedness in going after it was considered a bit strange. The child howled in response to the change in emotions around him and the mother looked down disappointed at her husband's seeming lack of good manners.

It was not until the following morning that my grandfather had come back. It did indeed turn out that he had forgotten a case in the train and that he had galloped after the train to retrieve it. He had had to ride the horse all the way to Artesia, the next station, and even then he had nearly missed it. Of course, a case of clothes was important, but the sheer panic that had seized him had been fuelled by the knowledge that inside the case was a very special present for his wife. The first set of earrings he had ever purchased. They had been almost as expensive as the hoe! He had gone past the shop at least ten times before he had had the courage to go in to make the purchase. It had been a whites-only shop, so he had made sure no other customer was inside and had waved the money at the shopkeeper as he entered the store, so the man would be enticed to do a quick business before he could get into trouble. He had long understood that the shopkeepers cared more about the money than the colour of the hand that handed it over. A black hand just had to be quick, to avoid trouble for both of them.

When he went to the horseman to return the horse, and to offer a chicken by way of an apology, he was too embarrassed to tell him the real reason behind his panic. He decided to say that his passport was in the case.

But that evening, in the privacy of their rondavel, my grandfather had produced the pair of gold earrings and shown them to his wife to admire. He had then removed the old crooked ones she had always worn, and fastened the new gleaming ones. He had next produced a small mirror he had bought on the trip, and gave it to his wife to admire herself. My grandmother says she is certain she became pregnant that night.

She wore the beautiful earrings for many years and they were admired by all. She was even nicknamed Mmagauta, mother of gold, affectionately, by her mother-in-law. The name stuck and she named the child she conceived on that night she first wore the earrings, Gauta. Then, at her husband's funeral, she was wiping her eyes which would not stop filling with tears, when she swiped the right earring off. That is when she decided to put it away in the chest. She could not bring herself to fasten it back on.

'So Nei, I knew all along where that earring was. Now, will you put it on? I'm giving you both. Wear them for me. Make them sparkle with your beauty. Please, child of my child?' How could I refuse my grandmother?

The chest yielded other treasures: a photograph of my grand-father as a young man taken at a *kgotla* meeting, a knife with an intricately carved handle, a pair of male sandals that had curled up and could not possibly be wearable, an arrow head and a *kgotla* chair. My grandmother told me of the significance of each item. She seemed to want to say everything all at once. She was not giving the story in instalments as she had often done. And where, in the past, she had been the one to insist that we stop and that I go and help with errands, she had been keen to go on. She went on, long after supper had been served and the family had given up trying to get us out to join them. It became dark and we had to light a paraffin lamp, but still we stayed in and talked and told stories long into the night.

One evening, Noka and I were sent off to the lands to check on the family goats, an errand that did not make sense since a neighbour had been asked to do just that and no word had been received that there was any problem with the arrangement. When we came back a day later, it was to learn that grandmother had failed to wake up that morning. And, almost as if on cue, my mother had gone and had a new baby!

CHAPTER 15

'Rra-Monei, tell me about the cattle post. You were gone a long time.' My father was usually called Rra-Leruo, that is, by his eldest child. But I always called him Rra-Monei, by my own name.

'What do you want to know, my child?'

'I want to know about the cattle and the animals. I want to know about the lion that killed a cow last year. I want to know who cooks for you at the cattle post.'

My father humoured me. He almost always did. He told me about the cow with the broken horn and the horse that threw my brother Noka. He told me about lions roaring at night and the hyena that killed a small goat. He did not, however, tell me about the matters that had weighed heavily on his heart during the three months of self-banishment. I knew I was too young to be the recipient of such information but even as he spoke to me, his mind seemed to be some place else.

Years later, with my bags packed for my first trip to the United Kingdom, and with my first and never-used passport lying on my lap, he told me about his three months of confusion. He died a year later, before I qualified as a architect. How I wish he had lived longer! Sometimes I just have to sign a cheque or document and memories of my father flood my head and heart. I think of that proud signature that he appended to official papers to get me my first passport. I think of that last night I spent with him, before I flew off to architectural school. The night he told me he loved me, without even articulating it specifically. The night he opened his heart to me. I think back and I remember, imagine and fill in the blanks.

'It's not the baby's fault!' he had screamed silently to himself. 'I can't reject an innocent baby. It's not her fault.' But how could he raise a Dutch child after the bad things the Boers had done to his tribe for years? Hadn't they had to leave their prime land across the Madikwe River because the Boers had attacked them? Hadn't the Boers had their Chief thrashed like a commoner and a criminal, humiliating the entire tribe? Now he had a Boer for a grandchild. A coloured grandchild. How could he love her? Weren't the Boers arresting anyone who dared to challenge their evil laws? Weren't they fomenting trouble across the sub-region, setting brother against brother?

But there was a competing consideration. There was a personal story that kept on leaping to his conscience whenever he thought about his grandchild. He had grown up with loving parents, Mfafu and Lelegaisang, and six siblings. He had been the proud first-born, the chief of his own small tribe. Then one evening, at end of his initiation ceremony, when he had come home swelling with pride at finally being a man, his father, Mfafu, had sat him down and told him a story he could never have imagined in his wildest dreams.

'My son, Tsietsi, I have something to tell you. You are old enough to understand, for you are now a man.' There was a resignation in his father's eyes he had never seen before. But still he, Tsietsi, a swaggering young man, was expecting another long speech about what makes a man and the importance of the family.

'I am ready to hear your counsel, father. I promise to listen and never to bring shame to the Ntuka name.'

'You will never bring shame to the Ntuka name. You are the son every father dreams of. But yes, it is names and totems that I will tell you about. This is the story of your life. It will shock you, but please listen and take it like a man. Don't interrupt until I am done. Your aunt Naniso is your real mother. Please don't interrupt. Please, my son, let me expose my heart to the wind. I know you will have many questions, but listen to me first. Yes, aunt Naniso, my own sister, is your mother. This is what happened.

'Your mother, my beautiful sister, was married late in life. And she did not immediately have children. She was sad about that and she was starting to despair when, finally, she became pregnant with you. There was great jubilation in the family when the news became known. Her husband, your uncle Bobatho, who is your real father, killed a cow to celebrate and fatten his pregnant wife. He went out to get load after load of firewood, to keep her warm. He killed a white goat and had beer brewed to thank God and the ancestors. Everyone waited with unmitigated happiness for your birth.

'You were born on a calm moonlit night. Your aunt, that is your mother, came back here to have you, as is the custom with first-born children. So it was my mother, her mother too, of course, who was the midwife. I myself had just taken a wife, your mother, I mean the mother who raised you. I listened to the news of your coming with joy. My first niece or nephew was on the way. And I had hopes that my wife was already pregnant. I remember the night so clearly. Your father was at his own ward, waiting for word of your birth. I remember hearing a jackal howling from afar as I waited anxiously at the ward *kgotla* for news of this long awaited child.

'I must have dozed off, for I was startled to hear footsteps coming my way. I raised my head, cocking it, hoping to catch a baby's cry. Why do they arrive annoyed, when the world awaits them with such hope? Anyway, my wife was hurrying towards me. There was fear in her steps. They were not steps of joy.

'"My husband," she whispered, "I have bad news. The baby is a *setlhodi*. Yes, he has an owl imprinted on his belly! The mark of evil, right on his tiny belly!"

'"A *setlhodi*? An owl? What do you mean? Please, my wife what are you saying?"

'"I am saying the child is marked! A beautiful baby boy, he is. But on his belly is the mark of evil. What will we do? Your mother and your grandmother want to return him as is the custom. To silence him before your sister sees him."

'"Return him? You mean kill him? What do you mean before my sister sees him?"

'"The birth was hard for her. She passed out at the end. But we have to act soon. I am afraid my husband. You must come and help?"

"'Help? Help? What do you mean help? *Setlhodi?* What are you saying?"

"'My husband, are you okay? Are you listening? Come! Hurry! You must help your mothers to make a decision. Quick! Now!"

"'*Setlhodi*? That can't be. An owl? Who would put a curse on one so precious? Haven't we all waited for this birth? For this boy? What will his father say? Do? I mean how can that be? A *setlhodi*? How can that be, my wife?"

"'My husband! I must insist. Please come. Maybe they have returned him already. Isn't there something that can be done? Can't we call a doctor to protect the baby? To release him from the evil?"

'I rose as if in a dream and followed my wife. With fear gripping my heart, I walked into the rondavel where your mother lay, exhausted from bringing you into the world. I was a man entering a woman's world, but that was hardly uppermost in my mind that night. I demanded to see you and my mother handed you to me. What I remember is the warmth of your body. And your fragility. And your little persistent heart. I examined you and I have to say that owl's face staring at me from your tiny belly unnerved me. But I took one look at your face and I knew that I would defend you with my life. I was willing to face and fight any evil.

"'What should we do, my son," my mother asked.

"'Of course, there is only one thing to do. We must return him. And you should not be in here. This is our job," my grandmother answered with a sad resigned tone.

'I looked at my wife, whose eyes were fixed anxiously on my sister, as if willing her not to wake up before a decision was made.

"'The child will not be returned," I announced.

"'What! You will bring ruin to all of us. A child born cursed must be returned at once. You should not be in here at all! We should not be having this discussion. We should have silently returned the boy by now. Your mother has no backbone. As for your wife! How could she bring you in here!"

"'This child will be allowed to live. If ruin comes to all of us, then let it be so! We will not spill an innocent's blood to save our own. Let there be rivers of blood, if that be the wish of God! Now continue with your work."

'My mother said a prayer for all of us. There was fear in that room. But there was also relief. You started to howl and I placed you on your mother's breast.

'Of course, we called a diviner to help. He helped us call upon your ancestors for protection. At first, he thought you should have been returned but, throwing the bones, he was sure that a compromise could be reached. And he was able to call the owl out. The treatment was hard on you. But you were always such a good baby. Such a tough little thing. You cried very little and you healed fast. Soon the owl was gone. Only a scar was left where it had been. But the compromise with the ancestors was that my wife and I raise you as our child. We had intervened for you, the diviner said, so the ancestors would expect us to be responsible for you for the rest of your life.

'Your mother, that is your birth mother, was so confused by all this that, at first, we thought she had lost her mind. But she saw the wisdom behind the compromise. She did not want to lose you altogether, so she agreed to love you from a distance. It has been painful to watch sometimes. She had two other children after you, your cousins, Tebatso and Naledi, but still you are her first-born, and she never did have another son. I have seen her watch you with longing. It has been hard sometimes.

'I am telling you all this because now that you are a man, the secret serves no purpose. You must know who you are, if you are to marry and have children of your own. You will always be my first-born. You will always bring happiness to my heart. And I speak for the woman who raised you as well. Now, my son, I have unburdened myself, only to burden you. How you deal with this, will be an indicator of my success at raising a first-born.'

Alone at the cattle post, my father had recalled that conversation as if it had taken place only recently. He had recalled the tears he and his father had shed together. He had recalled the conflicting feelings that had overcome him that night. He had felt anger, gratitude, love, abandonment and fear. He had also felt relief at finally understanding the tensions he had felt over the years between his birth mother and his mother. With his own personal history, how then could he possibly reject Dutchgirl?

'Ewetse,' he had whispered to himself. 'That is the name I give to my grandchild. To signify that my heart is at rest.'

That was the story he told me later. At the time, after absent-mindedly humouring me with superficial stories, his attention had returned to the present and he said to me, 'Nei, my daughter, I can't sit here all day telling you stories. But if you come with me on the donkey cart, I will tell you more stories on the way.'

'Where are you going on the donkey cart? And what will Mma-Monei say?'

'I am sure we can convince her to let you come with me. Bring your schoolbooks. You can do your homework in the bush as I collect firewood.'

I had looked at him skeptically. Books belonged at school and were taken home only to facilitate the doing of homework. Even during the longest of school breaks, I had never taken my books to the lands. They certainly did not belong in the bush. I could almost feel lashes raining down on my back at even the suggestion of taking my books to the bush. But my father was already getting the donkey harnesses together and acting as if taking books to the bush were a very normal thing. I was just as curious as I was anxious.

Within minutes we were leaving the village behind in a two-wheeled home-made cart being pulled by Selinah and Kante, the family donkeys.

'You promised me another story, Rra-Monei. Will you tell me about *bogwera*. Will you tell me what happens at initiation school?'

'You know I can't tell you about that! Both of us would go mad if I did.'

'I don't mean the taboo stuff. I mean the other stories. How you hunt and sing. How you live in the bush for a whole month. What you do during the month there.'

'Nei, all that is private! That is the taboo stuff! You know that!'

'Okay then, what about *dikoma*, the special songs. They are beautiful songs. Why can't we sing them? You sing them at the main *Kgotla* but we can't repeat them afterwards. What would happen if we did?'

'Nei, you are asking questions that even a fool would not ask. You don't even want to think about singing those special songs. Is that what going to school is making you into? A perpetual questioner? Come Nei, ask a question that can be answered.'

128

'How does *thobega* work? How can a broken bone be mended by putting all that stuff on the flesh? I don't understand!'

'Are you planning to be a diviner now? Is that it?'

'No, Rra-Monei. I just don't understand, that's all.'

'You would have to be a diviner to understand so, since I am not a diviner or God, I can't help you. Do you want to know how your mother and I met?'

'You will tell me? Really?' I was excited.

'I will tell only if you promise not to tell your mother that I have told you. And I have something to ask of you as well. And you can't tell your mother about that either.'

I looked up at my father who had brought the cart to a stop and was steering the donkeys off the road.

'Nei, my daughter, you have been in school now for five years. You must have learned a lot by now. Do you think you could learn how to write my name, and then teach me? Can you look it up in your books and teach me.' The request came as a complete surprise for me. I had never even thought it possible that my father would be interested in holding a pen. I looked at my father and was filled with confusion. The idea of my father writing anything was so alien it was slightly frightening. And, I was not sure I was capable of teaching anyone how to write. But then I saw the embarrassment in my father's eyes and I answered, 'Let's alight and find a comfortable spot Rra-Monei. I will teach you how to write your name.'

'I want to sign my name, not thump-print the forms, when I receive money from your brothers at the mine. Is my name in your books? Can you learn it and then teach to me? How long will it take? You have been in school for five years. You must have learned many things by now.' I had never seen my father so animated before.

'I don't need my books to teach you to write your name. Why don't we write in the sand? That's how I learned during my first year in school.'

'I brought some papers to practise on. Here.' Shyly, Rra-Monei removed several sheets of brown paper from his pocket. Paper was precious so he must have been hoarding it for weeks. Why don't you write my name down, let me study it and see if I can't copy it out.'

I agreed that that was the best way to start. Teaching my father the entire alphabet, only to select a few letters to make up his name did not seem like a good use of our time.

Over the next month, we made up all kinds of excuses to be together. We went to look for the donkeys, a job normally reserved for Noka. We walked together to see an ailing aunt. All to gain some private time. During these private times, I learned about how my parents had met and then married, over the initial protestations of my mother's parents, and my father learned to write his name.

Within two sessions he had decided on a way to remember the letters that made up his name, Tsietsi Ntuka. For his first name, he decided that T looked like the cross on which Jesus was nailed, 's' a snake, 'i' a finger and 'e' an eye. Thus by the end of the month, all he had to do was whisper to himself 'Jesus, snake, finger, eye, Jesus, snake, finger', as he painstakingly wrote out Tsietsi. For his surname, he would whisper, 'The funny chair, cross, the cup, the axe and the face.'

'Why is that Jesus?' I had asked, pointing at the letter 't'; at first, not understanding.

'Didn't they nail Father James' ancestor, Jesus, to something like that? I'm sure they did! Or at least that is what Father James says.'

'Oh! I see. Now that we are finally done, I think it is time for the final instalment of the wedding story.'

'All right, you must listen carefully, because in my story, in everyone's story, there is always a lesson. If you miss the lesson, then you might as well have blocked your ears to the story. Your mother was and still is a beautiful woman. Remember she was also the only girl in her family. Her family was rich and owned beautiful cattle and *difala* overflowing with grain. Their home was the best decorated. They were proud of their hard work and wanted to make sure that their daughter married into a successful family. I have already told you that they had a young man already marked out for her. No agreements had been reached but the mothers had whispered and suggested enough so that it was only a matter of time before the matter was resolved.'

'But I still don't understand why they objected to you and your family. You've told me that your family was well respected. Didn't your father kill a lion when he was only a young man? Hadn't you cleared a whole extension to your field only months after your initiation?' I had been raised on stories of my father's family's hard work and honesty. My mother was always reminding us that we carried the blood of honourable people in our veins.

'The reasons, my child, were never openly discussed. They had to do with things that had happened a long time ago. My name, Tsietsi, meaning confusion and indecision, tells a story I can't tell you today. Perhaps one day, when you are older, I will find the words to tell you. Let us just say that I was marked at birth, in a way that filled your mother's parents with fear. I didn't blame them for their objections, but I was still determined that I would marry your mother. But your mother, your beautiful spoiled mother, cried and threatened to run away if her parents would not agree to our marriage. Finally they relented. But as the wedding approached, and she was placed in confinement, cut off from me, I was scared. What if they forced her to change her mind? What if they married her to the other man secretly? What if he stole her, with the connivance of her uncle? Her uncle had been adamant that I was unsuitable as a husband for his niece. All he had to do would have been to arrange for the other man to steal your mother, take her to his home and declare themselves man and wife the following day. As long as her parents endorsed the theft, a marriage could have been declared. The man's family would just have had to pay the *bogadi* cattle and that would have been the end of us! Those were four long excruciating weeks. So you can imagine my relief when the day of our marriage finally arrived. It was the happiest day of my life.'

There was silence for a while. I had plenty of questions, but before I asked the first one, he added, in a tone that suggested that our conversation was over, at least for the moment, 'But for you, Nei, your future will be different. Independence means new things. New challenges, my child, which need new skills. That's why we sent you to school. So that you can have the tools to meet this new wind that is blowing. We don't even know if it is a good wind. Perhaps the English got tired of this dusty, barren place. They never built roads or tall buildings here like they did in Rhodesia or South Africa. Rhodesia I have never seen, but I have seen Gauteng with my own eyes. It was the gold that made them love South Africa so much. But we, my child, have no gold, so the English didn't bother much with us. It is for us, for you, to meet the challenge. And school is how to begin.'

'Rra-Monei, sometimes the teachers are so harsh. They lash us for no reason. They lash us for getting things wrong, saying they are encouraging us to try harder. They lash us for getting things right, saying that will teach us never to slip up. Some of the teachers can cause one to flee from school.'

'I know my child. I know. But what can we do? Schools are where teachers rule. How can someone who can't write enter a school and tell the teachers how to run their business?'

I looked up horrified at the thought of my father intervening on my behalf. 'No, no, Rra-Monei, I don't want you to come to our school! That would make things worse. Oh, that would certainly make things worse.'

'You have to persevere, my child. You have to try your best and stay in school. Who knows where you could end up with education?'

A year after this, my own mother, seemingly totally out of the blue, had a baby. I was shocked and angry. This unexpected baby seemed promptly to be loved by everyone. As if that was not enough, everyone started calling my mother Mma-Keletso and my father Rra-Keletso. My siblings did not seem to mind at all. Even little Dutchgirl, who was a toddler by then, loved the little baby. I felt betrayed by my parents and everyone. No one seemed to realise the unfairness of my being displaced, without so much as a warning. I was angry for a year as I felt that my father had been pretending that I was special to him, while in the meantime, he was planning this ultimate betrayal. After that I called my parents *mme* and *ntate,* never, never Mma-Monei or Rra-Monei. And certainly not Mma-Keletso or Rra-Keletso.

My grandmother had died and I had no one to talk to. To feel close to her, I made one of her flannel underskirts into a night-dress and wore it the whole year. When one of the straps broke I mended it and when my mother so much as touched it, a dark rage engulfed me.

A month after the birth of Keletso, when my mother was still in confinement, I chopped down a tree and made a pole, then dug a hole near the entrance of our yard and planted the pole in there. To this pole I nailed a metal plate I had made. On the plate was my name. All this I did by myself, refusing to answer questions and definitely refusing any help. When I was done, my hands were blistered, I was covered with dust and I was hungry and thirsty. But I refused food and took a secret sip of water at the back of the yard. And as long as my pole, bearing my name, was planted at the yard entrance, everybody who came to visit talked about me before they asked about that usurper Keletso.

There were times when I would look at my baby sister and try to vapourise her with my stare. Then just before she turned to dust, she would start to cry and something that felt strangely like love would tug at my heart. Then I would pick her up and if no one was looking I would cuddle her and hug her and sing her a lullaby. I knew I didn't love her so I would be confused by my desire to comfort her. This would make me angry and I would march over to my mother and declare that Keletso was deaf and no lullaby could ever soothe her.

I had even, when Keletso was on the breast, secretly hopped around on one shoe, with the hope that one of my mother's breasts would fall off. I should have been old enough then to know that the story that wearing one shoe would cause your mother's breast to fall was just a ploy to encourage children to look after their shoes. But I was desperate. My plan was to cause one breast to fall off and then the other, so Keletso would not have a breast to latch on.

It really seemed to me that my parents whispered to each other and laughed a lot immediately after the birth of Keletso. They seemed to find everything the child did funny. They laughed ridiculously loud when she slid on her tummy instead of crawling like a normal baby. And when she sprinted and fell, instead of taking careful steps like any other child, they laughed and told everybody who came to visit about it. It was all stupid, in my view.

It was when I was still in this angry mood that yet another family meeting about 'the Rhodesian affair', as my father had dubbed it, was called. I was watching the children, Dutchgirl and Keletso, at Mma-Gopane's yard as the adults assembled. As their discussions progressed and I heard bits of it, I started to fantasise that perhaps the Rhodesian girl's mother would take me away from my parents. I created this image in my head of a mother saddened by the prospect of losing her own daughter. I imagined the Rhodesian family arriving in a ox-drawn wagon, the mother of the daughter weeping pitifully at the imminent loss. As the wagon stopped, an uncle bundled out a howling girl, while the mother covered her face with a shawl, tears streaming down her face. Her tears were the colour of milk; rich and creamy. As the girl was frog marched towards my waiting relatives, the mother peeped from under her shawl, saw me and asked in a small voice, 'Will you not give me this unloved one? I will love her as my own.' In my daydream, I ran towards the woman in the wagon, the twelve magnificent oxen sprouted wings and we flew away, leaving my cruel relatives behind.

My fantasy was blown to bits by my mother's voice, 'Nei, Nei, are you listening? Go and clean Kele's face. Make her blow her nose. Are you listening to me?' Without meaning to or knowing that it was going to happen, I started crying. Hot tears that rolled down my even hotter face.

'You don't love me any more,' I screamed. 'You want to give me to the Rhodesians. I know you do. Kele! Always Kele! Every day Kele! Why don't you give her to the Rhodesians! She is an ugly child anyway! I want to die and be with my grandmother!'

Then I ran back home leaving a stunned silence behind me. When I got home I took off my clothes and put on my special nightdress. I took out a blanket from my grandmother's chest and spread it over a mat on the floor. I crawled into bed and covered myself, although it was a hot mid-morning. I cried until I thought I would die from grief and loneliness. I don't know when I finally fell asleep but when I woke up it was late afternoon. I was hungry but I had decided to starve myself to death. 'Let them suffer with guilt when I am dead and gone,' I thought to myself.

'Nei, my child, please come with me to collect firewood.' My father was standing at the door of the rondavel, his gentle eyes regarding me. I almost jumped out of bed with happiness, but then I thought, 'He thinks I am going to fall for that trick. He already has a youngest child. He does not need me.'

'I beg you to come, my child. I have a story to tell you. Will you not come?' Still I did not move.

'And you need to finish your grandmother's story. She died before you finished telling it, didn't she? I will listen. Come, my child.' My heart did a flutter, as if there was a dove in my chest. I thought I was going to start crying again but instead I got up. I put on my dress over the nightdress. 'Bring the blanket, my child. We might need it if we are late coming back.' It was my grandmother's special blanket and it most probably had never been taken out of the rondavel, except to be washed. It definitely had never been taken out into the bush. My father had to very remorseful to suggest such a thing. I eagerly grabbed the blanket and walked towards my waiting father.

CHAPTER 16

The sun was about to set and my father drove our donkey-cart into the sunset with me next to him. Even Selinah and Kante, our usually playful donkeys, seemed to sense the tension behind them. At first, I resisted the urge to snuggle. I was still afraid to love him, in case he did not love me back. I was thinking to myself that I was no longer the last born and that my mother would not be coming to live with me in her old age, as was our custom. Keletso had displaced me from my special place in the family and I had not even been consulted before my whole reason for being had been upturned. Noka, being the last male child would inherit my family compound. My older brother Leruo would inherit the cattle post and the management of the family cattle. I was just another middle child, with no special place in the family. Keletso had taken my place. She would inherit the family field and, most importantly, she would inherit the honour of taking care of our mother in her old age. 'Nei, you are my last-born girl child; you will empty my chamber pot when my knees are too old to let me get up before sunrise,' my mother had told me many times before the birth of Keletso. I imagined her whispering this to Keletso and my head was ready to implode with jealousy. As my eyes brimmed with tears, my father pulled me up to him and pressed his lips against the top of my head.

'When Leruo was born, I felt a pride and happiness I had not known was possible. I was no longer a boy. I was a man! Of course, I had been told I was a man at my initiation but, by having fathered a child, I had proved it. It is said that God made man in his own image. Well, I felt a bit like God, I had made a person in my own image! I loved Leruo. No doubt, you will learn this when you have your own children. I love each one of you. But each child demands a different type of love and therefore gets a different type of love. You, I loved you through singing and talking to you. Being alone with you. Listening to you. Telling you stories others would not have valued. Perhaps the birth of Keletso interrupted this. Of course, it did. She too demanded to be loved. But she did not take your love or in any way reduce it. Do you understand? You will always be my special Nei. My little storyteller. Didn't you teach me how to write my name? Come Nei, tell me the rest of your grandmother's story.

'How did you know?'

'Come on, you don't make people in your own image without knowing a thing or two! Okay, she told me. Before she died she said to me, 'That little Nei has a gift. Make her finish the story of my life. She must remember it for her daughter.' She made me promise to listen. So will you tell me the rest of the story?'

As the western sky exploded with colours and the eastern sky offered what it could in response, I told my father the story of his own mother. This was, of course, before I knew the story of his birth.

As I looked at his soft face, at this man who was a great *dikoma* singer, at this man who was a great praise poet, at this man whose arms and legs were ripples of muscle, at this man who had made me in his own image, I loved him so much it hurt. I recalled the story of how he had met my mother and how they had courted and married.

'Your mother was the most beautiful girl in the village,' he had told me. 'She comes from a family of beautiful women.'

'All of them, the most beautiful in the village and your wife the most beautiful of them all?' I had teased.

'Yes, of course, how did you guess?' I had giggled happily in response.

'Her parents were against our marriage. With hindsight, I don't blame them but, at the time, anyone who dared question my right to marry her was an enemy! An instant enemy.'

'What do you mean, you do not blame them?' I had asked.

'Oh, Nei, that is a different story all together. A story is like a river; some tributaries must be saved for later navigation. Let's keep to the main channel, my child. I'm sure I have told you that before. Anyway, my uncle cautioned me: 'A beggar must be patient. Don't ram your head at a wall whose thickness you are not sure of. Tap on it, listen to it, smell it. But don't smash it.' That is what he said to me. I was young and strong-headed. Above all, I was petrified that some other young man would end up marrying your mother. I mean, the thought that I could possibly live without her filled me with fear. I thought of all kinds of schemes. Perhaps I could make her pregnant so that her family would feel obligated to let me marry her. But she was not having any of that nonsense. For months, as the family discussed the matter, I was paralysed with fear. Then, one Sunday – I know it was a Sunday because the Dutch Reformed Church had just started ringing that annoying bell every Sunday – my uncle came to tell me, 'They have agreed,' he said. 'Who have agreed?' I asked. I didn't want to hope too much so I asked, even as I thought I knew, what he was talking about. 'You can marry her. You can marry Marato. It has been agreed, you can marry her.'

'I tell you, my daughter. You are there, I am here; it is the honest truth that I leaped into the air and said the most heartfelt praise poem in honour of your mother. You have heard me praise the Chief, a new bride, a cow before milking, but I promise you I have never felt a praise poem well from my heart like the one I said on that hill that day.'

'What kind of day was it? Do you remember?' I had a thousand questions, but I didn't want to break the spell of the storytelling. Yet I wanted to keep him on the main channel. The tributaries could wait for later navigation.

'I can tell you everything about that day, my child!' But instead of describing the day, he launched into a praise poem.

'"Whose child is she?" they ask. They ask because they see a diamond in the sand. They see a star throbbing in the darkness. They see a rainbow and wonder if they can keep it for next summer. They see milk and wonder if they can steal its whiteness. They see light and they wonder if they can feel it in a hug. I hear cascading voices, asking the same question, "Whose child is this?" "Need I answer," I retort. Who else could have produced this gem, this diamond? But the Chief is asking, "Whose child is this?" Tribes are asking, "Whose child is this?" I say to the Chief and all the tribes of the world, "Need I answer? Is it not obvious? No other womb but the womb of my wife, Marato, could have possibly carried this star." They say, "Arrogance does not fit you." I say, "This is not arrogance speaking, people of my tribe, this is the naked truth; only the womb of my beautiful wife could have brought forth this beauty. She is Monei, daughter of Tsietsi and Marato. Tsietsi, the praise-poet and *koma*-singer. Marato, the great dancer, whose movements made young men forget their own names. I saw her dance and was filled with lightness. I will praise the Chief, for am I not but a servant of the tribe? I will praise my nephews and nieces as they take their places amongst adults. That is my duty. But no praise poem can be sweeter than the one I said on that hill, for my then bride to be! For I am Tsietsi, the son of Mfafu and Lelegaisang. Mfafu, the son of Mosu and Pelonomi of Mosibudula Ward. Mosu who is the son of Borekhu. Mosu the Brave, who was of the Maunatlala Regiment. Borekhu who, during the three-year drought, dug a well at Tauteng, saving the entire tribe. Borekhu who smashed in the face of a hyena with his bare fists."'

My father had paused, a smile played on his lips, his eyes glistened with fond memories and he grabbed me and crushed me to his chest.

'Nei, my child, you asked about the day,' he had continued after a while, with still the smile playing on his lips. 'It actually started off as a strangely angry day. Dark clouds, *matlakadibe,* gathered. I watched them rolling and snuffing out the light. I thought to myself, "This can not be a good sign." I thought perhaps it is a sign from my ancestors that I should give up my dream of marrying Marato. It was with these thoughts going through my mind that I saw my uncle struggling up the hill. His face appeared to be contorted with annoyance, but it turned out that he was merely struggling with the demanding slope. And as soon as he told me the news, the dark clouds dispersed and gentler, fluffy-white clouds gathered. Later a gentle rain fell, feeding the earth and blessing our marriage. My uncle hurried back down the hill, seeking to avoid the rain, but I continued to sit up there and to let

139

the warm wetness engulf and encase me. A yellow butterfly joined me, landing on my left knee. With my hands clasped over my knee to shelter it from the rain, the two of us enjoyed minutes of silence and watched a rainbow that could only have been an omen. I wondered about what the butterfly was celebrating that day. A recently discovered flower? The rain? A newly hatched clutch of eggs? Perhaps a caterpillar that had just been transformed into a beautiful butterfly bride.

'When the rain stopped, the yellow butterfly flew off to its life and that is when my heart spilled open and I said what I know to be the best praise poem I have ever recited. No one but the rainbow, the white fluffy clouds, my God, my ancestors and perhaps the little yellow butterfly heard it.'

My father brought me back to the present, as he gently urged, 'Tell me the story of my mother, your grandmother Lelegaisang.'

'She used to tell me that as long a story has a teller, it has no end, for the teller's own story becomes part of the tale. She made me promise to tell my story to my children, especially to my first daughter and then only if they promise to pass on the story to their own children.'

'Yes, I know, and she thought you were a great storyteller. She used to say, "That little Nei of yours may be the worst basket-weaver I have ever tried to teach, but she can weave words and moods like no other. She will take our memories to the next generation." I know she was right. So will you tell me the story of her funeral?'

'But you were there. And I don't want to remember that sad day. In any event, that is not the story I promised to tell my daughter!'

'Nei my child, remember what your grandmother used to say. A story has no end as long as there is a storyteller to tell it. And, of course, you will have to tell that story to your own children. So will you tell it to me? I may have been there, but no two hearts can see the same thing. Tell me, my child. I'm listening. Look, the *kopadilalo* is waiting for your story too.'

I looked up, and true enough, Jupiter was blinking in antici-pation of my story. I snuggled up to my father and started, 'She always smelled special, my grandmother. But that last week I think

140

I knew something was not right. She was not slower in her movements or sick-looking in any way, but she smelled really strong. It was like she was emptying herself out because she would not be needing herself anymore. Am I making any sense?' I looked at my father and he was nodding.

'And her eyes had an intense sparkle. It was like she was feeling and wanting to be felt more than ever before. I felt specially drawn to her that week. One day, I pretended to be ill, just so I didn't have to go to school. On yet another, I simply refused to go. Usually, she would have insisted I go to school but she did not.

'One night we sat, the two of us, just like we are doing right now, watching the stars come out. She used to tell me that no one should ever be too busy to acknowledge the first star of the evening. That night she quietly named the stars as they popped out of the darkness. Then they popped out so fast she could not keep up. She laughed her special laugh and then she fell silent. As if thinking deep thoughts. Then she pointed out some stars and asked me to name them. I didn't do so well so she admonished me in a very gentle but firm voice, 'Do you care at all that the sun comes up every morning to warm up your day, to give you life? Do you care at all that the moon and the stars beautify your nights? Do you care at all that the rain makes you and the trees grow? Do you care that a rainbow will pop out, just to make you happy? Nei, child of my child, you must care, for nothing is forever. Promise me that you will learn the names of the stars and you will know when the full moon will rise. Promise me that you will make a wish when the full moon rises.' I nodded in the darkness but I was choked with feeling. It seemed to me that we were talking about more than just names of stars and the cycle of the moon. Then she continued, 'Nei, child of my child, the heart will remember long after the head has forgotten. It is things that touch your heart that will sustain you long after the things that entered your head have evaporated. The head will hear whatever the ear hears, but the heart is more selective. Things that lodge themselves in your heart are things that will sustain you forever.'

I muttered my agreement but I did not understand everything she was saying. I was even a little scared. My grandmother had told me many things, some I was not even supposed to know, but her tone was totally new. And her smell was over-powering me. I felt like I was inhaling her, like she was physically, but lightly, tapping at my heart. Like she was consuming me, or perhaps me consuming she. My heart was melting in a way that made me want to cry and be comforted. For the first time ever, I wished I could remember the taste of my mother's breast milk. I wanted to curl up somewhere deep and warm and comfortable. But instead I felt that my grandmother was coming into my body, my soul, my heart, my womb, even. I had never felt I had a womb until that day. Not in the way that women have wombs in which babies grow and later get born. I wanted to shout that, of course, stars were forever and that the full moon would always rise and that the sun was obligated to rise and set. That was the way of nature. But I was not feeling so certain of these truths that night.

'Grandmother, I do care. I really do care,' I whispered desperately.

'I know you care. I know you care, little Nei. Let's promise each other that if one evening, *kopadilalo* decided not to rise, that if you and I looked up and it was not there, we would not agonise night after night about its absence, but rather we would be thankful that it had been there in the first place. That we will remember the joy it brought us, and not dwell on the sadness of its absence. Of course, we will mourn it, but we will be thankful that we had it to gaze upon. Can we promise each other that, child of my child? Because, I promise you, too much sadness can drown good memories. You see, sadness and happiness are both matters of the heart. And sadness is very good at crowding out happiness, especially if the happiness is based on memories.'

My grandmother and I made the pact that if *kopadilalalo* did not rise, we would not dwell on the sadness of its absence.

My father drew me up to his chest and whispered, almost fearfully, 'And little Nei, have you kept your side of the bargain? Have you not let sadness crowd out happy memories?' At this I cried and cried and cried. My father let me, only holding me, but otherwise saying nothing. When I couldn't cry any more, I whispered into the darkness, 'I love Keletso. I really do.'

'I know you do. Your mother knows you do as well.'

142

'I miss my grandmother.' I had not said the words to anyone since my grandmother died.

My father's voice was very gentle as he responded, 'Of course you do. But her story will never end, because you will tell it and others will tell it. And it has grown in your heart where nothing will ever crowd it out. Not sadness, not time, not distance.'

Then I said with an urgency that I had not thought I felt, 'I really, really, love Keletso. I really, really do!'

'Of course, Nei. Your grandmother died and then Keletso was born. Remember that sadness is good at crowding happiness out of one's heart. Let's go home, before you mother sends out a search party.'

'Can I tell you a bit more? Let me tell you about the day my grandmother and I opened the chest. Will you listen just a few more minutes?' I wanted to relive that afternoon and my father granted me my wish and listened as an impossibly red moon sliced through the eastern horizon. I leaned against my father's chest and I gave voice to the love and loss that I had felt for the past months.

Then I asked in a whisper, 'What did you decide about the Rhodesian girl? Is her family going to give her up? Is she going to be Uncle Rra-Gopane's second wife?'

My father pulled me closer and whispered into my hair, 'No Nei. We have decided that we can't bend to the customs of others. It is not our custom to take a human being as compensation for the death of a member of our family. So, the answer is no. We will not accept the Rhodesian's offer.'

'I'm glad Rra-Monei. I have had sleepless nights dreaming about this whole thing. But tell me, is Rra-Gopane disappointed?'

'No, no, no! Nei, Rra-Gopane is not disappointed. He is man who has lost his only son and, of course, he very briefly entertained thoughts of siring yet another when this Rhodesian matter was first brought up. But even he knows that that would have been the worst solution. This young girl would have been a constant reminder of how his son died. He might even, without realising it, have wanted to possess a member of his killer's family, for revenge. To own her and punish her. But in the long run, that was never a good solution. So, he too is happier that the matter has been decided once and for all. He has many daughters and one of

143

them will bear him a grandson one day. It is just a matter of time.'
I thought to myself, my family is not into taking other people's
children, so they are unlikely to give away their own. But still
I asked, 'Rra-Monei, if it were our custom, and if Leruo or Noka
had killed someone else's son, would you give me away? I mean
to the victim's family to be the wife of some old man? Would
you?'

'Nei, Nei my child! I would die before I gave you up. No matter the custom! No matter the law! No matter the consequences.
Look at me, my child; am I telling you the truth?' I looked at his
face in the moonlight and I knew without a shadow of doubt that
he was telling me the truth. I decided then that I didn't have to
worry too much about the possibility of being circumambulated by
Berka Solomon, whatever that meant, if I didn't feel like it.

Later, we rode home in silence because I was fast asleep. My
father was watching the road by the aid of the moon, which had
risen not just to beautify our night, but to guide us home.

CHAPTER 17

It was my last year of primary school, my seventh. It should have been Standard Five but, just as the Queen had years ago decided that centimetres were preferable to inches, the new government had decided on a new way of numbering primary school standards. Instead of the original Sub A, Sub B and the Standards One to Five, they had decided that Sub A would be called Standard One. I was thus doing Standard Seven. My teacher, Mr Khunou, was even more feared than Mrs Monyatsi. He had joined the school two years before and already it was said that Mrs Monyatsi and Mr Moile were angels in comparison. The only good thing that had happened to our class was that Shadrach, the bully, had dropped out of school to go to the gold mines in South Africa.

A new class bully, Mokoko, had emerged, but he was more of a bumbling fool with a nasty temper than a really mean person. He was, in truth, rather slow but covered it up by threatening violence to anyone who seemed about to expose his slowness. Once, during a science lesson, he was able to see, in a drop of dam water, among other large water animals, a hippopotamus, and this through a microscope lens. True, we were all excited, our class being the first ever to use such an expensive piece of equipment, but a hippopotamus? We could not stop laughing and even the teacher allowed us to go a bit wild. Come lunchtime, we had to pay with food. Mokoko was gluttonous, which Father James said was a sin, so we piled his plate with some of our maize porridge to make him happy and with the hope that he would end up in hell. It seemed only fair that he should end up being fried and eaten by Satan since he seemed eager to eat everything in his path. He would hastily cup the porridge with his not-too-clean hands, brown milk running through his fingers and down his arms, and shovel it into his eager mouth. Everybody else, on the other hand, would mix the porridge and the milk, to encourage the worms to float to the top then scoop them out, or as many of them as would, before eating. We might even add water, if there was not enough liquid to encourage the bugs to float to the top. If we could not get rid of the worms, at least we closed out eyes as we ate. Mokoko didn't bother with these worm reduction and avoidance exercises. He ate everything with unmitigated relish.

We had seen Mokoko cry once and that made him seem much more human than Shadrach had ever seemed. Mr Khunou had asked a trick question, which most of us knew not to answer, even at the risk of being ordered to kiss our desks. 'There is a kraal full of cattle, how do you single out the bull? One word only!' 'I would see the difference with my own eyes! I've herded cattle for many years, teacher!' Mokoko hooted without even bothering to raise up his hand. He was hardly ever confident he had the correct answer but this was a question he was certain he could answer.

'One word, I said!'

'Eyes.'

'I didn't know a bull's eyes were different from a cow's eyes! Try again, Mokoko.'

Mokoko scratched his head and thought about the question. Mr Khunou lowered his voice conspiratorially and urged Mokoko not to be shy.

'Testicles!' Mokoko whispered, wide-eyed. He could not believe he had just been granted permission to use such a bad word in class. But Mr Khunou snorted in response, 'Oh Mokoko, I didn't know you used your testicles to find out the sex of your father's cattle! So what do you do? You expose yourself to the cattle? Come to the front of the class to show us how you use your testicles to tell bulls from cows.' Mokoko broke down and sobbed. Most of us had known about the trick question from the previous year's class. A girl had once accepted the challenge and uttered the word only to be invited to show her testicles to the class. 'Oh what a strange girl you are? You have testicles? Let's see them!' She had been so mortified that she had refused to go back to school. Only after a whole year out did her parents succeed in persuading her to go back to school. She agreed to go back as long she could go to a different school. In the end she had to walk twice as far to school and to repeat a standard.

For some reason, which was related to the fact that he was having children with his wife as well as the wife's younger sister, which practice produced cousins-cum-siblings that looked like twins, Mr Khunou did not live with the other teachers within the school compound. Instead he lived in a compound which he shared with his large family just behind the village granaries. Apparently the school inspectors did not approve of Mr Khunou's marital arrangements.

It was also rumoured that Mr Khunou and his family ate cats, a rumour that was both supported and disputed by the fact that their compound was crawling with cats, even black ones. 'Why would he have so many cats? He must eat them.' 'Why would he still have so many cats if he ate cats?' Having children who were both siblings and cousins was bad enough, but having your yard crawling with cats, and many of them black, and possibly eating them, was something else. So even if he had not been a vicious teacher, which he certainly was, he was still not the sort of person one could like. There was evidence that neither of his women liked him too much either. They were rather quiet and reclusive. Their yard, from what Mary and I had observed one day, when we peeped through the bush fence, was crawling, not just with cats but children as well. Children at all stages of development, it seemed to us. We didn't tell anyone at school. A story like that could fly through the school in no time. Then next thing you know, Mr Khunou is interrogating you.

Mr Khunou rode a bicycle to school and, unfortunately for our class, one cold June morning he was crossing the river when he and his bicycle fell in. He rode on to school, hoping that his clothes would dry on the way, but the winter sun was not strong enough.

Twenty minutes later, he peddled into the schoolyard with mud streaking down his clothes and shoes oozing water. Most of us erupted in laughter upon seeing the seemingly humbled Mr Khunou through the window. We were to be rewarded for our reaction calmly and meticulously.

First Mr Khunou parked his bicycle and went into the classroom, whereupon the laughter stopped abruptly and we all sprang to our feet to acknowledge his entrance.

'Good morning, class,' Mr Khunou called calmly.

'Good morning, Mr Khunou,' the class responded.

'Good morning, class,' Mr Khunou called out calmly, once again.

'Good morning, Mr Khunou,' we responded with more verve.

'Good morning, class!'

'Good morning, Mr Khunou.'

'It is a good morning, is it not?'

We were not sure how to answer that one. It was a new greeting. When we did not respond Mr Khunou asked the question once again. So we responded, 'It is a good morning, Mr Khuno!' He seemed happy enough with our response. He nodded for us to sit down and we silently did so.

Then Mr Khunou went out, retrieved a bucket and a cup from the kitchen area, filled the bucket with water, and carried the bucket and the cup back to the classroom. The whole class was watching, wondering what was to come next. Was he going to wash his muddy bicycle? Was he going to clean his shoes? Why was he not ordering a student to get the water? These were silent questions as none of us dared speak out loud. Mr Khunou walked and placed the bucket of water on his table. I was beginning to think that perhaps Mr Khunou was ill.

'Kiss the desk,' he called. We understood this to mean that we should place our faces on our desks. This always meant lashes to the back and although we didn't think we had done anything wrong, that was no reason not to expect lashes. But, as I tilted my head and stole a peep to see which row he would be starting with, I saw that it was not lashes we would be receiving. Mr Khunou scooped a cupful of water, walked towards the row closest to the door, pulled back Martha's dress around the neck and then emptied the cup down her back. He went back and forth, scooping water and pouring it down the backs of all the pupils until he had dealt with all forty or so of us. It was a cold Monday morning. I was bare kneed, without socks and with toes peeping from old, torn shoes. My little cardigan had hardly been sufficient to keep me warm to begin with, now I was soaking wet. The night had been so cold that I had woken up with cold feet from a dream in which my feet had died and gone to heaven leaving me with stumps to hobble to school. After that, sleep had been difficult and even though I limited my morning ablutions to washing my face, legs and arms – those parts that would be visible to teachers – the cold water made me shiver even more. Still, like everyone else, I remained quiet, forehead glued to the desk until Mr Khunou ordered, 'At ease. And first lesson this morning is English Spelling. Get your books out.' Mr Khunou was still calm. Dangerously calm, I thought.

I was shivering which I was afraid was going to interfere with my concentration. We all knew that even the best in the class could not cope with the speed with which an annoyed Mr Khunou rattled off English words in a spelling test. I was listening but Mr Khunou only grunted non-stop. I stole a look sideways and I saw that everyone was frozen, pens poised over exercise books. The class waited for the words but Mr Khunou was grunting strangely. I was looking at my poised, newly acquired pen and thanking God and my ancestors that I had realised that I had lost my pen and had done something about it before class started. One did not find out such critical facts after Mr Khunou started class without suffering some serious consequences. On finding out that I was without a pen, I had offered half my lunch to anyone with a spare pen to trade. At first, there were no takers, then Thomas offered his for the whole of my lunch and I had accepted the offer just as Mr Khunou had become visible through the window. There had been no time to negotiate. He had tossed the pen at me and now I was ready for Mr Khunou's spelling test. But Mr Khunou was grunting. Perhaps he was ill after all.

'Okay, pass your books,' Mr Khunou growled.

There was fear as realisation dawned. The grunts were the words to be written out.

'Maureen, go and get my stick! I am going to teach these nincompoops a lesson.'

Maureen's eyes clouded over. She did not want to go but she had to. Mr Khunou followed her out of the classroom. The storeroom was just next door to our classroom, but they were gone a long time. Maureen came back first and her eyes were cast down. Mr Khunou followed a few minutes later; his trousers were a bit rumpled, his face was sweaty and he was breathing strangely. 'Let me see your backs, NOW! Sweaters off! Kiss your desks! I will teach you to laugh at your teacher!' We took off our sweaters and we all leaned forward and Mr Khunou rained blows up and down the six rows. I was certain my dress had been sliced open. I could almost smell my own blood as Mr Khunou moved to the next person. Only Maureen was spared but she was crying anyway. Whatever happened in the storeroom whenever Maureen or Sylvia got sent there was not very pleasant.

'Out!' Mr Khunou shouted. 'Ten laps around the football pitch. I want to hear you say, "I am stupid and I will end up nowhere! I will never laugh at my teacher!" I want to hear you from here! Now out!'

We all trooped out. Maureen was crying more than everybody else. No one looked at her.

'Why are you so hard on them?' Mrs Masie had come from her class to talk to Mr Khunou. Mrs Masie was perhaps the nicest teacher to come to Lady Locklear Primary School. Once, when I had been thrown out of class and ordered to go back home to wash my face properly, she had called me to a storeroom and with a wet hankerchief she had cleaned my face. She had then rubbed Vaseline on my face and arms. Afraid that Mr Khunou would know that she had interfered, she had made me wait a while, so that it would seem like I had gone home to wash. And when once I had, after taking off my *makgabe,* put on my school uniform but then forgotten to put on my school panties, she had discreetly whispered the information to me. I had been in Sub B at the time and she had not even been my teacher but she had taken to trouble to warn me of my unfortunate state of undress. I had been mortified and had not played at all the whole day, but I had been eternally grateful to Mrs Masie. I really liked her.

'I don't interfere with your class, so please don't interfere with mine!' In response to Mr Khunou's bark, Mrs Masie ducked back into her class. She was not good at confrontations at all.

Mrs Masie had a son about my age who would have been in our class had he been attending our school. But when she could not have him moved to another class, Mrs Masie sent him to live with her brother and his wife in Kanye. She had tried to play dodge Khunou the previous year, and had hoped that she could keep her son home this year. She had thought that Mr Khunou would continue teaching the same standard, but Mr Khunou had been promoted to teach Standard Seven. So Mrs Masie's son was going to have to spend yet one more school year away from home. Mr Khunou had been heard muttering about women who raised weak sons and sent them off to be taught by some weak teachers in far off villages.

My classmates and I headed for the football pitch, a sandy patch, to amuse ourselves.

As I ran, keeping to the middle of the group, I wondered why God didn't take Mr Khunou or at least make him a bit ill so he would miss a day or two of school. I said a very earnest and silent prayer that he be struck by lightning right at that moment, but the sky remained blue and the cold breeze continued relentlessly. God seemed to take good people, never the likes of Mr Khunou. God had just taken my brother's new-born baby daughter. My heart went out to my brother, Leruo, who had missed two very important events in his twenty-five years of life.

First, he had missed his own wedding. Two months before he had left for South Africa to work at the gold mines, he had fallen in love with Selemo, a beautiful girl two wards away. He had been so in love that he had considered not going to South Africa. Our father had intervened.

'A man who changes his mind at the smell of *makgabe* will not go far in life. Go to the mines my son. Make money and come back and marry your beautiful girl.' It had been sound advice so Leruo went to Johannesburg; Gauteng, the place of gold. Close to a year later he wrote, or rather, he dictated a letter to a friend, to say he would be home for Christmas and he wished to marry his sweetheart during that time. Arrangements were made. His family entered into negotiations with Selemo's family. Dates were set. Cattle for *bogadi*, bride wealth and the feasts were selected. Beer was brewed. Dresses were selected. Banns were published. Then Leruo wrote to say his leave had been cancelled. His bosses would not let him take leave. It was too late to change course, so the families agreed that someone would have to stand in for Leruo. A cousin was selected, and so it happened that Madisa appeared before the District Commissioner and pretended to be his cousin Leruo. The family saw no reason to apprise the District Commissioner, a white man who they believed would not have understood, of the true position. If he detected sadness in the eyes of the bride, he probably put it down to the seriousness of marriage. He quickly pronounced the couple 'man and wife' and retreated to his office where, it was rumoured, he kept a bottle of whisky. It was said that his ever-glazed eyes were a result of the repeated swigs he took from the bottle in the top left drawer of his desk.

Mr Summerhill, a young white man who had recently arrived in the village to work at the District Commissioner's office, emerged from his room and, out of pure kindness, snapped a picture of the newlyweds. He smiled at the sad couple and promised that the photograph would be ready in a month's time. He would be going to Mafikeng to have the many photographs he had taken developed. The sad new wife, hearing mention of a town in South Africa, whispered to her uncle that perhaps the white man could say hello to her husband for her. An aunt ordered her to lower her eyes, as a bride should, and the uncle barked that the white man was not to know that the man next to her was not her husband. The bride lowered her head and a lonely tear rolled down her left cheek.

Mr Summerhill kept his word about the photograph. My father kept the picture and the marriage certificate safely for Leruo, who was not able to see his new wife until a whole year after he married her by proxy. When he did arrive, our father called a few aunts and uncles and, under their watchful eyes, he was presented with his wife and the two documents proving the marriage. Leruo thanked his cousin and nodded at his new wife. There was, however, no sparkle of gratitude in her eyes. Instead there was cold sadness.

Later on, when he was alone, Leruo cut out the picture of our cousin and taped a picture of himself where the other had been. He placed the new creation in a frame and hung it in his rondavel. He also framed the marriage certificate and hung it up. He had spent close to two hours painstakingly making the two frames.

By the time he left for South Africa three months later, his new wife was pregnant. But the little girl died within three months of her birth. Before her father had even seen her. He came a few months after the low-key funeral and he and his wife made a bed over their dead daughter, buried in a small clay pot under the floor of their rondavel.

I had seen the sadness in my brother's eyes and had wondered why God would want to take a beautiful innocent baby, before her father had even seen her, when there was Mr Khunou. Granted, Khunou had a wife, sister-in-law-cum-wife and eleven children, but even they did not seem to be happy to have him around. And Father James was always on about Satan and how he was after those full of sin! Didn't Mr Khunou personify sin itself? I certainly thought so.

'Hurry-up! I don't have the whole day! Come on hurry-up. Move it!' Mr Khunou called to us to come back. We struggled back to the classroom. Tired, cold and hurting. Maureen was still crying. Her crying was not the more common sniffing, squirming pain-induced crying. It was a silent face-down-hiding kind of crying. Maureen was one of the older girls in the class and she was big and usually in charge in the playground. Her crying was hard to watch, so none of us looked at her. The whole class shared the shame of the storeroom, even though not everyone really understood it.

CHAPTER 18

O f all the chores, I preferred water collecting because I could walk with friends, sing, read or just count butterflies as I went back and forth between home and the borehole. So, to me, water collecting was not really hard work. The downside of the chore was that it was when most fights took place, so that an old insult could be remembered and suddenly you are invited to settle the score. Often these fights were only to spice up boring hours. A few slaps and shoves and a winner was declared.

They were really no different from a decision to steal a watermelon from some field or even to ride a stray donkey. On one occasion, a brave soul had even convinced us to grab and milk a goat directly into our mouths. This was a dangerous activity as most goats had been fixed by a traditional doctor so that this kind of theft could result in very serious adverse consequences. The mildest of the repercussions was mouth sores but a child was known to have bellowed like a goat until he died an agonising death. His feet and hands had hardened into hoofs just before he died. Although the milk had been sweet, it was an activity I never repeated. I must have been out of my mind to agree to that escapade.

One day we were walking to the borehole with other girls from my ward. One of them, Mmoni, decided on a way to create some excitement.

'Let us check if the *mototo* is in,' Mmoni suggested. Her eyes were sparkling with mischief.

'Please leave her alone. You will get us into trouble again,' countered Kadimo and she broke into a run.

I hurried on, after Kadimo, as I too did not want to be part of tormenting Mokgela.

Mmoni had called her *mototo,* a barren woman. That word itself was so insulting that to say it aloud was both an act of courage and evidence of improper breeding. I had uttered it only once in my life and I had received a slap across my face that had left me dizzy for a few seconds. 'If I ever, ever hear you use that word, I will kill you with my bare hands. I did not raise you to use such words!' My mother was a believer that instruments other than bare hands should be used to punish children. A grass broom or a switch, preferably selected by the offender, were generally her instruments of choice. She considered slaps as an indication of loss of control on the part of the parent. To use one's bare hands, I had heard her say, was bringing the adult to the level of the child. My mother was not in the habit of losing control, so that slap was a constant reminder to me that *mototo* was not a word I could ever utter again. I did not want to hear it either. Adults were never too keen to hold inquisitions about who did what or to take time to apportion blame properly. They generally preferred blanket punishment to all those who were present during the infraction. Perhaps it was to save time. I had no intention of being present when punishment was being meted out for the crime of tormenting Mokgela, so I had to remove myself from the place of the commission of the crime.

I certainly understood why Kadimo was running away. The last time Mmoni had talked Kadimo into throwing stones at Mokgela's house, the woman's dogs had leapt over the fence causing them to flee through thorn bushes. Kadimo had ended up with a dented bucket and a lashing from her mother. We had all been told repeatedly to leave Mokgela alone but the fact that she lived childless, with only dogs for company, intrigued all of us children. We invented and recycled all sorts of rumours about Mokgela. One story was that she had actually given birth to the dogs, but sometimes the story was that she engaged in unmentionable acts with the dogs. One rumour was that she rode the dogs at night to get the children who had called her names or had thrown stones at her house during the day. According to this version, the dogs licked the offender all over the body during his or her sleep and the result was that victim would never have children. This was the scariest of the stories because none of us would know if we had been licked until we got married and found we could not have children. Then there was the story that she was actually a dog and that, if one had the courage to stop and look her in the face, they would see that she was actually a dog dressed as a woman. The stories changed all the time and were embellished by the tellers. The fact that Mokgela never left her compound or received guests, except for the two men who took care of her cattle at her cattle post, added fuel to our speculations about her life. The adults would merely say that Mokgela was the only child of a rich couple long deceased. The real story behind her seemed to be a secret known only to adults.

At the borehole, Rasesana, the man in charge of the place, Mr Borehole Pomper, as he insisted on being called, on account of the fact that he pumped water from a borehole, had decided that we had to wash the reservoir. He had half-filled the reservoir and he let us go in naked, to scrub its floor and sides. We liked washing the reservoir because we could turn the whole task into swimming, when he was not looking. And he was never looking, as there was a drinking place just across the river where he went when he was supposed to be at work.

Within minutes, the reservoir was full with screaming children, splashing around and doing very little scrubbing. We pushed and shoved and splashed merrily.

Then a fight broke out between two older girls about one hundred metres away. That was obviously more attractive than swimming in a algae-infested reservoir, so we jumped out to go and watch.

Now, Selela and Kolopo were known to be enemies, and a confrontation between them had been anticipated for weeks. Kolopo was rumoured to be conducting a secret relationship with Moses Shanko, a man who had been coveted by many of the neighbourhood females, until he had made his choice known to all. Moses Shanko had just arrived from the gold mines in South Africa. He had been observed purchasing a tube of Ambi, a skin-lightening cream, but the tube never reached Selela, to whom he was betrothed. Those who had seen Shanko make the purchase were certain that the cream had been 'Ambi for Women', so it could definitely be assumed that Shanko had not made the purchase for himself. He was light in complexion anyway, so he did not need any skin-lightening cream. The obvious conclusion was that he had given the Ambi to Kolopo. Kolopo's face had indeed begun to ripen to a yellowish colour and her close friends did say that she had not denied receiving a tube of Ambi lightening-cream from Shanko. For weeks this information had made the rounds, and for weeks we had expected some confrontational resolution. Selela was well known for her tendency to fight at the slightest provocation. In fact, Kolopo was considered either brave or stupid to be messing with Selela.

As I scrambled into my dress, grabbed my bucket and ran over towards the massing crowd, I knew that I would be in trouble with Mr Borehole Pomper and my parents for getting side-tracked while on an errand. But still, I was not about to miss a fight. Watchers were already making bets on who would win. School lunches, rubbers, rulers, pencils, skipping ropes, marbles and other valuables, were at stake. I decided not to make a bet. A loser may well give you a slap across the face a few days along the way for not having believed in her. I had seen it happen. In any event, I didn't know either of the participants enough to make an informed bet.

As I approached the crowd, I realised for the first time that an ant was digging into my right toe, sending a searing pain up my ankle. My first instinct was to squash it by grinding it between my left heel and the toe under attack, but I knew better. These were nasty ants. You killed one and dozens would attack you immediately. So I gently picked up the little ant and, making sure that I did not squash it, tossed it away. I was hoping it had not given off an alarm as I picked it off. I scratched my burning toe to get some relief and then ran off to watch the fight which by then, from the lack of sound from the crowd, was in full swing.

As I joined the crowd and elbowed my way to the front, the bucket serving as a useful weapon, I heard a scream from Selela and then blood erupted from her mouth. Blood was pouring out of Kolopo's mouth as well but she did not seem to be feeling any pain. She spat out something and wiped her mouth with the back of her hand. Whatever she spat out fell right into a cloud of milling ants. The stomping of the two women had disturbed them and they were already mad with rage, crawling around and not dispersing. Just as I realised that the bit spat out by Kolopo was a piece of flesh, in fact, a piece of Selela's lower lip, the ants massed around it and carried it away. There was a collective gasp of wonder as we all watched these tiny little ants carrying a part of a screaming but very alive woman, away into their hole. The ants had reacted so promptly, and with such co-ordination, as if they had been waiting for this very piece of lip their whole lives. Someone sprang forward to save the lip, but he must have realised the futility of the action. He kicked the cluster of ants slightly and the ants scattered, but promptly zeroed in again on their trophy. By then Selela was being led away and Kolopo was being given a very wide berth. Fighting over a boy was fine, expected even, but biting off someone's lip, even for a boy, was something else. She was no hero. She was a monster. Even her best friends took a circuitous route back home, rather than walk with their lip-biting friend.

I saw Mmoni hurrying towards Selela, with an extended hand. She was offering chicken droppings, for Selela to rub into the wound, so that Kolopo's teeth would rot and fall out. Selela was too distressed to think of revenge yet, so she ignored the extended hand. A friend took the chicken droppings and rubbed them into the bleeding wound. The blood continued to pour out, washing the droppings away. I wasn't sure whether that meant that Kolopo's teeth would not fall out or not.

'Selela's uncle is a witchdoctor. That Kolopo is in trouble, I tell you,' someone opined. Indeed Selela's uncle was known to be so powerful that he would not have to take Kolopo's excrement to maim or kill her; the sand where her footprints were would be enough. He had once caused an enemy to drown in a puddle of water so shallow that two cows had drunk up all the water within half an hour. His own cattle survived on a spring with no obvious source and no larger than a bowl.

'And now Shanko will have to marry Selela. He can't make his girlfriend bite Selela's lip, maiming her, only to walk away from her. Who is going to marry a girl with a deformed lip?'

'I didn't know Kolopo was like that! I thought she was a nice person. I am shocked!'

'Maybe we should have taken the lip for Selela's uncle! Maybe he would have worked on it so Kolopo goes mad or something. She didn't fight fair.'

'Shanko should be ashamed of himself! Look what happens when you sneak behind your girl friend's back.'

'I don't see how Shanko is to blame for the biting. For the fighting yes! But not for the biting. Biting is sneaky and dishonest fighting.'

'Well, he got involved with a biting woman. So he is responsible!'

'I'm sure he bought her the Ambi and maybe even that bra she was wearing. Did you see that she was wearing a new bra? I'm sure he bought it!'

'Where is Shanko anyway?'

'He went to the cattle post yesterday. He is coming back tomorrow and then he leaves for the mines.'

'I think Selela's father is going to show him the buttocks of a baboon! Mark my words!'

Advice, information and opinions tumbled out thick and fast. A few people even forgot to fill their buckets with water, but instead followed Selela home, wanting to be present when her parents learned of her maiming. Kadimo and I filled our buckets and walked back to our respective homes together. We were silent most of the time. I could still see that army of ants carrying a part of a live human being away. I imagined that part nestled in the ant hole, being hacked to pieces. Will they feast on the tiny pieces tonight, or will they save them for the winter?

The matter took months to resolve between the families of the two girls and that of Shanko. With the threat of Selela's uncle's powers always in the air, Shanko and Selela were married within a year. He made a special mid-year trip from the mines for the occasion. It was a big white wedding. The groom's family paid six cattle as *bogadi* and slaughtered two for the feast. The bride's family slaughtered three cattle, one goat and one sheep for the feast at their home. Selela's deformed lip trembled with happiness and she cried, as she was expected to, when her uncle chanted a praise poem about her.

Kolopo's family sent her off to live in Lentswe la Moriti, a village four hundred kilometres away. She found a husband of her own and came back to Mochudi for the wedding. Her wedding was a happy enough affair, but she would forever remain the woman who in her youth bit off a rival's lip. '*Chobolo*', people whispered behind her back.

As for me, that night I dreamed that all the village albinos, old women identified as witches, childless women, Eve, and mental retards had been rounded-up at the main *kgotla* for a public thrashing by Mr Khunou and Shadrach, with Kolopo, who was Shadrach's wife, cheering them on. Their whips lashed and slashed, leaving rivers of blood. In this strange dream, Shadrach was the President of Botswana, having taken over from Nebuchadnezzar, who, when he was full of fury, had ordered that Shadrach, Meshach, and Abednego be roasted in a furnace. Shadrach had walked out of the furnace unscathed. My dream was not clear as to what had happened to Meshach, and Abednego.

I woke up bathed in warm sweat with the howls and cries of the village's unfortunates still ringing in my ears. Then I leapt off my mat as I realised that, unless I hurried, I would be late for church. I had joined the Dutch Reformed Church *Phuthagwana*, and hoped to be baptised before the end of the year. I chanted the verses, from the Book of Daniel, I would be tested on on that day; two in particular, kept churning in my mind. 'And whoever does not fall down and worship shall be cast immediately into the midst of a burning fiery furnace,' Daniel 3:6 threatened. The *moruti* had repeatedly promised us that King Nebuchadnezzar's furnace, into which he had cast those Jews who did not worship his gods, would be nothing in comparison to God's fire in hell, into which we would be cast and roast for eternity, if we did not seek the shelter of the Lord Jesus Christ. It seemed pretty likely that I would end up in Hell, in view of the fact that I could never really believe in Jesus' special place in the scheme of religious matters. Try as I did to believe without questions or doubt, I could not. Was he really born to a virgin woman? Wasn't his overturning the tables in the temple a bit violent? And wasn't it rather rude for him to answer his own mother, as he reportedly did, according to the Book of Luke, 'Why did you seek Me? Did you not know that I must be about My Father's business?' I could not imagine responding like that to my parents. I also wondered and was rather unhappy about the absence of any black angels. The Dutch Reformed Church's heaven, as advertised by the reverend in flowing gowns, did not seem like a place where I could expect to meet my relatives. I wondered whether souls wandered around aimlessly unable to figure out where their bodies, raised from the dead, fitted into the eternal-life scheme of things. Was heaven organised into wards and villages or did it have straight roads called streets? What about the ages of the rising dead? Would they rise at the same age at which they had died? That could be problematic, as some people would end up being older than their parents! Aunt Sissy had died at twenty-two leaving three young children who were now grand-parents themselves! In my dreams, Serurubele could talk, but she had been new-born when she died. This tended to support my suspicion that one did not stop growing and aging just because one was dead. The *Phuthagwana* Teacher, a fierce-faced white woman, did not tolerate questions and I had been repeatedly told to learn my verses and repeat them when asked to.

'A mind that questions the Word of God, is a mind inhabited by Satan. Cast Satan out of your mind and your heart will be free of doubts. I can assure you, More-Nay, that greater minds settled these truths long before you were born, long before anyone of us was born,' I was admonished. Satan continued to occupy my mind and my heart could not be free of doubt and, as a result, I failed the *Phuthagwana* examinations and I was not baptised with my classmates. To avoid embarrassment, I disappeared to the lands as my *Phuthagwana* classmates made preparations to celebrate the big day. Their families threw huge parties and goats and chickens were slaughtered. I did worry about being roasted in hell by a garden-fork-wielding, long-tailed Satan but I did take comfort in the knowledge that, if indeed hell existed, I would not lack company. In fact, hell was going to be a rather crowded place, seeing as before the arrival of the missionaries, the entire continent of Africa, with the exception of perhaps Egypt and Ethiopia, had been populated by heathens and Satan worshipers. And there were those still stubbornly refusing to convert to Christianity, not withstanding the threats of everlasting misery. Where is Hell exactly anyway? Heaven, it seemed to me both Christians and the entire village agreed, was obviously up in the sky. You did not have to go to church to know that it was where one ended up after death – except that the missionaries had introduced Jesus as some kind of gatekeeper. But is hell next to heaven? Is there a wall dividing the two? Will we be able to hear the screams of the people roasting in hell? If you get tired of eternal life, can you like leave? I mean like die? Maybe commit suicide? Where will you go if you kill yourself in heaven? I tried to keep these thoughts out seeing as they were responsible for my not being baptised with the rest of my *Phuthagwana* classmates. I briefly considered enrolling in the Catholic Church's catechism class but the persisting rumours of the Kokoto Father's shameful praying habits stopped that thought long before it matured into any serious plan.

I have always had very vivid dreams. Sometimes I felt like I lived two lives: the day life and the night life of my dreams. Sometimes I felt like I lived both at once, slipping from one to the other and back again. Then sometimes I felt like I lived and dreamed all kinds of conflicting truths.

CHAPTER 19

There is indeed a beautiful dream that I have often. To this day, I still have that dream, but always there is something or someone new in the dream. After everyone has gone to bed, I exit the village by a secret western gate and enter another world, another village, by another gate, just above the one I have just left. This night village is just above the village I live in by day, so that when I enter it by its western gate, I face east. The sun and I make a pact to meet at the village above. The sun is just rising as I enter my secret village above my day village. It's a green place with wild marigolds and butterflies.

On one such journey, I pass by the village *kgotla* where young male initiates have just arrived from a month in the bush. They are being given their regiment name. They are beautiful, these young men with rippling muscles and proud faces. Mothers are beaming with pride and fathers are roaring into the hills, as they sing the *dikoma,* the special initiation songs. Sisters are proud but jealous of the special attention to the boys. They arrived a week before so their moment is over. Girls of marriageable age are standing on rock platforms, wanting to be seen but still shy, in case they are considered too forward.

Then I spot Kabo, his body gleaming with sweat from the marching and singing and acting that is part of the ceremony. He is standing, chest bare, muscles glistening, eyes focused ahead of him. A rock platform pops up from under my feet and, slowly, I am pushed up and elevated. I reach the same height as the other girls and, for a moment, I hover there. The voices of the men, young and old, thunder around me and I am mesmerised. Kabo is a respondent while Rra-Bina is the main lead singer. They are singing a song about going to war and wondering if they will come back. Rra-Bina's voice booms from one side of the *kgotla* and Kabo responds, and then the rest of the men join in. There is a rhythm that is enthralling. I get goose bumps as I stand there, clad only in a short skirt made from goat hide.

Then my rock rises above everyone else and I dance as Rra-Bina and Kabo sing below me. Suddenly, the sun is low on the horizon and I have to hurry back home, to the other village, my day village. I exit through the eastern gate, re-enter my day life through my secret eastern gate and wake to my mother's call. 'Nei, Nei, its time to wake up. You will be late for school.'

As I woke up and got ready for school, I forced my brain to recall the story of Cinderella and her wicked stepmother because we would be discussing it in class that day. I had had to read it in a hurry about five days before, and then had to give the book to Mary. There were four copies for the forty-strong class, and we had ten days within which the whole class should have read it. As I left for school, I asked my mother who or what she thought a Fairy Godmother was. My grandmother thought perhaps Mary, mother of Jesus was a Fairy Godmother, seeing how she was a mother to a half-God, according to Father James. She still maintained, however, that Mary's mother had given up too easily of Jesus' paternity. 'She ought to have pressed the girl,' she insisted.

Sometimes my journeys to the village of my dreams are less dramatic. I spend the day, perhaps I should say night, weaving baskets with my grandmother and my little niece, Leruo's daughter, who died at birth years ago, before she was even given a name. In my dream, she has a name – she is called Serurubele, meaning butterfly. It has to do with the fact that she is both beautiful and fragile that I gave her that name. Bele, I call her for short. She calls me Aunt Nei and it makes me feel all grown up. Sometimes I just walk the village footpaths, chatting with people, both dead and alive (to my day life), trading gossip. I drink an offered cup of milk, fresh from a goat and pause to play *morabaraba*, a type of checkers. I go off the footpath to pick wild berries; they are so plentiful that I hop from bush to bush, just sampling. I meet old friends and stop to chat and I also meet new friends. 'I am Monei, daughter of Tsietsi and Marato. Tsietsi the brave and Marato the beautiful.' There are nods of recognition all around and they too introduce themselves.

On one such trip my grandmother wanted me to tell her one more segment of the never-ending story of her life.

'I told it to my father. Weren't you listening, *Nkoko?* Weren't you listening?' In my dreams, my grandmother knew all about my day life, so I was rather distressed that she had missed my special trip with my father. What kind of ancestor was she if she didn't watch over me every minute?

'Of course I was listening, Nei, but you didn't tell him everything. Every story has many sides, like a diamond. Haven't I told you that often enough? A story can be told forever, not just because it grows and swells as it is told, but because the slant depends on the listener.'

Of course, my grandmother was right; I hadn't told her son everything she had told me. How could I have? The whole story would take a whole lifetime to tell!

'Go ahead, Nei, child of my child, tell me a story. The part you are to tell your own daughter when she becomes a woman.'

So up there in that secret village of my dreams, with little Bele delicately weaving a basket, I told yet another instalment of the story that I was yet to start and tell to my daughter who was not yet born.

'My grandmother's love for her husband was great, but that did not stop her from trembling with fright on the night of their wedding,' I began. My grandfather, Mfafu, was a big strong man. He came from a line of brave men. He could chop a load of wood at the blink of an eye. He could harness a span of twelve cattle with the help of only small boys. He could train and tame dogs. He had even tried his hand at taming a lion cub – he had the scars to prove it. He could fell a tree effortlessly. He had killed a lion in his youth and a leopard too! All that power was in my grandmother's bed and she was trembling. Could her love tame such force? Could kindness harness such power? She was excited and scared at the same time. She felt fragile thinking of his huge chest, his powerful muscles, his strong mouth, his black deep eyes. And there was that fascinating but frightening wedding night event still to take place!

'Outside their wedding night rondavel, drums rolled. Aunt Kese sang a love song. My grandmother heard her mother laugh in response to some joke and wondered, Are they already counting the months, hoping for a grandchild?

'But then my grandmother remembered: her new husband could do soft things too. He could sing – my could he sing! He could play the cow horn with such feeling that it moved women to tears. His father said he got goose bumps listening to him play. So my grandmother thought, It is Mfafu the singer who will lie next to me tonight. Not Mfafu the lion slayer. With this rationalisation, she was able to relax as she waited for her new husband. The men were taking too long with their last minute instructions to the young groom and my grandmother was getting anxious.

'When her husband finally came, Lelegaisaisang had fallen into a slight sleep. She thought that she was dreaming as Mfafu, her lover, had gently crawled onto the mat beside her. She felt a light touch on her waist. She felt a kiss on her shoulder. She felt nibbles on her right ear. Still she thought she was dreaming. Then she heard a murmur, "You are beautiful," the voice said. Then she was wide awake. What was she supposed to do? She had been to initiation school so she had been taught to respond to a man. To kiss back and give pleasure. But they had not prepared her for this storm of feelings. These feelings of wanting to flee and wanting to be ensnared at the same time. This melting of her heart and her womb and her liver and her head! This helplessness she felt. She felt like a puddle of milk; sweet, pure but on its own helpless. She felt light and feathery. My grandmother remembers that, on that first night being with her husband, she felt like she was flying, soaring, floating, drifting, exploding, throbbing and imploding. She said she felt so many things, some of them contradictory, that I would laugh and say, "*Nkoko*, can you make up your mind about how you felt?" "Not so loud Nei! Or I will not tell you any more," she would caution.'

'Nei, child of my child, Bele is tired, and you have to go now. Will you tell me more next time you come to visit?' And indeed little Serurubele, with a face just like my brother, who had never seen her, had slumped over her great-grandmother's lap, basket still in her right hand. She was breathing steadily. I bent over and kissed her on the forehead, kissed my grandmother on the lips and bid them farewell. I had to hurry because the sun was setting and would no doubt be rising in the village of my day life. But before I left, I asked a question that had been uppermost in my mind, 'Nkoko, what if I can't have children? What then? Who then will I tell all these stories to?' My grandmother smiled at me and said, 'Nei, child of my child, you and I are merely two beads in an intricately woven necklace. Look at your uncle Thono who never sired a child of his own. But doesn't he have children with his lovely wife? Didn't his brother step in to help, to make sure Thono can walk with pride amongst his peers? There will never be man or woman without children, as long as he or she has relatives. We are all one blood, child of my child. Now go on. Hurry.' I did have to hurry and I did.

CHAPTER 20

My sister Keneilwe, who clearly had eyes for Supang, the widower with starving goats, ended up marrying Seileng Batho, a man with a reckless past and the latest shoes from Johannesburg. It would appear that a one-time encounter left her pregnant and really neither of them wanted to be married. Seileng reckoned he had an adventurous future ahead of him and Keneilwe reckoned she would be happier with a rural man with a kraal full of goats. But she was quickly realising that pregnancy has a way of involving others and taking the decision of whom one wishes to marry out of one's hands.

At first, Seileng had denied the quick and furtive encounter in the field when Keneilwe should have been chasing away birds from eating the sorghum. His father must have believed him because, when they came to our yard to discuss the matter, he was rather puffed up at the beginning of the discussions. He was leaving for a long journey, he announced rather curtly, and was hoping that this unfortunate accusation would be dealt with without too much waste of his time. His attitude was that his son was a Johannesburger and it was unlikely that he would be interested in a girl who had not even bothered to lighten her skin or wear red lips.

Seileng, handsome and ramrod-straight, shoes shining and the latest Johannesburg jacket in place, was wearing a rather disdainful smile when my uncle put the allegation to him. But he soon crumbled under questioning, and that was when he tried another defence. Even his father was not impressed, for it was he who responded with disgust at such foolishness.

'My son, my son! Please don't make an already bad situation worse!' He was almost shouting. 'You have already sent us around the moon and sun! You have made me look like a liar in front of witnesses. Don't try to make me look foolish as well! You see all these men here, including myself? We are experienced in these matters and we all know that there is no way that any man is going to pull out at that critical time. We have been consumers of this thing for many years and, I dare say, you would not be here if I was not an expert on these matters! How can you claim that at the very point that God and your ancestors answered your prayers, you said no! That you pulled out! Please my son, don't insult these assembled fathers of our tribe! When a dog is dead, it is dead. To deny the obvious is to bring shame on those you are talking to.'

The ward headman, who had been called to help decide on the case of Seileng's denial of Keneilwe's pregnancy, offered, 'We are hearing very strange claims these days, indeed! There was a young man at the *kgotla* only five years ago. The son of Kukeke Raboladu, of Mosanteng Ward, it was. When he was confronted with a belly the size of this house, he sprang a third leg! His claim was that he had used a sheath, a cover called a penis rubber. A French envelope, I think he said it was called in Johannesburg. I had to warn him that if he went about admitting to pushing strange things into women like that, he was bound to be in trouble with the chief! What a scandal! It's one thing to come back from the mines with money, and a double bed and to entice some naïve girl to open her legs to you, but is quite another to wrap yourself in some contraption and push it into her! Really! The things modern people will get up to! We kept the matter from the chief. That young man could have ended up in real trouble!'

My uncle Rra-Kuki, who fancied himself to be knowledgeable on a wide range of issues, had replied, 'A French envelope? I have to say I know little about the French. I knew an Italian once and, if Italians had such envelopes, I dare say I would have heard about it. But certainly the English don't engage in such strange behaviour. You can say anything about the English, but you can't say they are into French envelopes and such strange things. Yes, you can't say that about the English. Civilised people, the English.'

Seileng was asked whether he wanted to pay for the collapse of

Keneilwe's breasts, or to marry her. Before he could answer, his father answered for him. His son would marry Keneilwe, he said. It was Seileng's second time to cause the collapse of a young woman's breasts and his father was not about to pay yet again, unless he was getting a daughter-in-law in return. If cattle were going to leave the Batho kraal once again, a wife was going to be acquired in return, this time.

One of Seileng's uncles commented, 'A man who laughs at a maiden will be her groom! It's for you now to work hard for this woman, feed her, clothe her, provide shelter for her and make her your diamond. Let it not be said that your wife is the thinnest in the village. Fill her with babies and be happy together. The days of going with this one and that one are over, my nephew. You are now a man, not a boy. May you be blessed with countless children.'

I have to say that my sister and her husband have been very happy together. They now have five beautiful children, at different levels of postprimary education, and you would never think that there was a time when a claim of coitus interruptus had threatened to keep them apart.

CHAPTER 21

A t the end of my seventh year in primary school, I sat for my Primary School Leaving Examinations – PLSE, it was called – and got all As. Those As paved the way for me to secondary school and later architectural school.

My brother Leruo gave me my first tube of Ambi Extra skin-lightening cream as a present for passing my examinations. My mother took it away, declaring that I was still to young to wear skin-lightening creams. 'It should be two more years before you even think of boys! And then make sure the thinking goes on for more years without you doing anything about it,' was her retort. But she was very happy at my results and she bought me two heavy blankets. For the first time ever, I would not have to share bedding at night. I was extremely happy. This started a ritual between us where my mother would buy me two blankets whenever I passed an exam. Even thirteen years later, when I was living in an electrified flat with running water, in Gaborone, and had a bedroom of my own, my mother bought me yet two more blankets for finally qualifying as an architect. My father gave me a cow to rear, declaring that I could take it and its progeny to my new home when I got married in years to come. He also slaughtered a goat for us to celebrate. My sister Keletso apologised for having chewed my rubber. I hadn't known what had happened and all along she had been worried that I was going to fail because of her. I picked her up, although she was really too old for that and told her that I loved her, which I did. I was asked what I was going to study after high school and I said I would study for a BA. My mother wanted to know what kind of work I would do with a BA and I said office work in a government office. 'But doing what?' my mother wanted to know. 'What Rose's father does in Gaborone,' was my answer. My mother had smiled uncertainly and my father had pronounced that there was ample time for me to decide what I would study after high school. I still secretly wanted to be the Queen.

My brother Noka was so impressed by my results, and the fact that I was going to high school, that he decided he wanted to go back to school. A group of missionary wives had just started a school for special needs children and children too old to enter the main school system. At first my father was reluctant, 'Who would look after the family cattle?' he asked. He would have to make alternative arrangements for the herding of the family cattle but Noka insisted. He wanted to learn how to read and write so he could speak English and perhaps one day buy a tractor and a double-bladed plough. 'Then I'd plough bigger fields and take better care of the cattle. I would know what to feed them and how to read the information on all those medicines that the government says are good for cattle. I too want to go to school.' Times were changing and my father was persuaded.

Amongst my classmates who did not write their exams was Martha Molebatsi. Polite, short-sighted Martha, who hardly ever said a word in class but almost always had everything correct in her neat clean handwriting. Obedient Martha, who was always on time for school and who never forgot her broom and who would single-handedly sweep most of the class if the girls in her sweeping detail were horsing around or dragging their feet. Martha, who having found out what a barrister did, had decided to change careers. She had decided she wanted to be a doctor for animals, a veterinary she said it was called, of all the strangest professions in the world, and had adopted a baby donkey, one of the least loved animals in our world. Martha, who once silently passed me her rubber as she observed me rubbing a hole into my exercise book with a wet finger. Such holes were fairly common, as were crooked lines, as we could not always afford such expensive learning tools as rubbers and rulers. But such holes or lines could earn one a serious beating so a surreptitiously passed rubber or ruler was a great favour, especially because if caught, the person passing the rubber or ruler could well end up in trouble herself. Martha, who listened to the BBC World Service at 8 o'clock every Saturday morning.

Martha had been one of my main, if quiet, competitors right from Sub A. We had even, early on, physically fought over that first position in class, although we had both pretended it was over a rag ball I had made and she had unravelled. She said she had unravelled the ball to remake it as it had lost its tightness and I said she had no right to decide when my ball needed fixing. Then she had, rather unexpectedly, slapped me across the face and I had slapped her back. We had grappled, doing very little harm to each other, and when the bell rang, marking the end of the morning break, we had separated with relief. At the end of that term, we had tied in first place and that had cooled the animosity between us.

Just two months before the final exams, Mr Khunou was swinging his whip about in frantic anger, hitting at random, when the point of his stick came into contact with Martha's right eye, puncturing it immediately. Within days it was confirmed that Martha was blind in her right eye. She dropped out of school and spent weeks in and out of hospital. There was talk that she was going to get a marble eye as soon as the hospital could get one. In the meantime, she would have to wear a scarf around her ruined eye to hide from curious stares and to protect it from the elements. Within weeks of the injury, Rra-Koketso, a kindly, forty-something-old man recently widowed, offered to marry the unfortunate girl. Who else would marry a *mogapa,* a one-eyed girl, but a widower with young children to be taken care of and more in his loins waiting to be made? Martha's parents accepted Rra-Koketso's offer without hesitation.

In all, about fifteen percent of us went on to secondary school, amongst us Mary and Berka Solomon. Berka, it seemed, was no longer given to perambulating in the geographical vicinity of our yard, and I cannot say I cared too much about this lapse.

ACKNOWLEDGEMENT

I want to acknowledge my dear friend Peter Dow for his very valuable comments and insights.